Ripples in a Pond

John Cannell

ISBN 978-1-913663-21-6

Printed by Biddles Books, King's Lynn, Norfolk PE32 1SF

Author's Note

When I started volunteering for Essex Wildlife Trust at Warley Place, fifteen years ago, I had no idea that it would lead to anything other than spending one morning a week doing odd jobs there, helping to maintain this lovely historic garden and wildlife reserve in a way that would suit both visitors and wildlife alike. It certainly helped to keep me fit, but also resulted in some valued friendships – not only with fellow volunteers, but with Willmott enthusiasts from all over the United Kingdom and beyond. This all resulted from passing one day on one of the manned open weekends and going in to find out what it was all about.

When I wrote the first Warley Place novel, *The Wall*, I thought it would be a single book, and was surprised how many were sold and how much people liked it. A reflection on what visitors thought of Warley Place, I thought, rather than the novel. Pressured into writing another, I produced *The Walnut Tree*, which also sold very well. But that was it. Another one would be boring. What else was there to say? Well, the phone calls and emails arrived – when is the next one coming out? I explained that there was little new to say, but eventually gave in and decided to write about what I have said above – how sometimes quite small things can change your life, then the change in your life changes someone else's, and so on. Hence the title. But this is the last one of a trilogy. No more.

As before, the events are mostly fictional. However, during my researches I became very friendly with members of the *Association pour la Sauvegarde du Patrimoine de Tresserve*, a lovely group dedicated to researching and preserving the history of the French village of Tresserve, where Ellen Willmott bought a chateau and where she visited regularly. At one stage, when her financial position was particularly dire, she did in fact consider selling Warley Place and moving to Tresserve. Two of the chapters recount events that are very similar to my own visit there, and the *Association's* later visit to Warley Place.

The characters are of course mostly fictional. The exceptions are: Ellen Willmott of course; her butler, James Robinson; her alpine gardener Jacob Maurer, and his wife Maggie. Ellen Willmott is usually portrayed as prickly and dominating, but researches have shown that there was a caring and thoughtful side to her character so I've tried to bring that out.

The volunteers are not based on any one volunteer, but an amalgam of them. Hard working, knowledgeable, good humoured, interesting people.

As before, the story is set in two time frames. One is 1934, the year Ellen Willmott died; the other is the present day. I use the term 'present day' loosely, because so much is happening at Warley Place that I couldn't keep up with the changes. In particular the noisy but incredibly useful contraption used to pull the heavily loaded trailer has, much to our regret, been set aside for Health and Safety reasons.

There are so many people I would like to thank, that you would never bother reading the list. All my fellow volunteers, my French friends, various research groups, friends who have proof-read the manuscript, visitors to Warley Place who have encouraged me, but perhaps most of all my wife, Shirley. I seem to have spent an enormous part of my life either at Warley Place, or up in my study working on musty old archives or writing this book, and she has never once complained. I know what my fellow volunteers would say. 'She likes you out of the way, John.'

I do hope you enjoy reading it.

1

Walking Home
May 1934

As the trail of steam pointed the way to Shenfield and the rattle of carriages faded, Ellen Willmott took a deep breath and put one foot on the first of what now seemed to be an interminable number of steps rising up from the platform of Brentwood Railway Station to the street above. Irritated with herself, she put one gloved hand on the handrail, her soon aching arm providing the much-needed assistance that her well-worn knees required, to make her way aloft. She rested for a moment at the half way mark; the other passengers had all passed by, some pausing to see if she was in need of help but then quickly continuing on their way. Maybe it was the look she gave them, perhaps the clothes she wore, she neither knew nor cared.

She liked London – apart from that affair with Galeries Lafayette all those years ago. Hadn't paid for it indeed! Did they really think she hadn't given the money for a scarf when she'd put all the others on her account? She had only noticed it on her way out and had bought it then. She was sure she had paid for it; she must have done. Did they really expect her to keep a till receipt? Anyway, she'd won the court case, that had shown them. The niggling thought in her mind that perhaps she might have over-reacted pushed away, she brought herself back to the present. It had been good to be with the choir again, but the day had been tiring and the hour was late. Robinson had many times pleaded with her not to make this final stage of the journey home on her own, especially at night, but showing any sign of weakness was simply not in her nature. She valued her butler. In fact, he was hardly just a butler now, more of a friend, who had reminded her of her years just once; never again. Seventy-five now, she firmly believed that age was all in the mind. Well mostly, she thought wryly as she eventually reached the top and carried straight on to the exit.

Emerging out on to the street she stopped for a moment, sighed, and thought again about how she used to enjoy journeys in the brougham. Her brow wrinkled. Why hadn't she told the coachman to meet her? Did she still have a brougham? Did she have a coachman? She suddenly couldn't remember. She'd got rid of the car, she remembered that, it was always breaking down. A couple passed by and glanced at her, frowning. She gave them one of her steely looks and they smiled at each other and walked on. Turning, she pulled her coat tight and started on her way up the slope towards Great Warley and her home at Warley Place.

It was a journey she had made many times on foot over the years. The summer sun had disappeared behind the houses on the far side of the road, the moon had not yet appeared and the first stars were pricking little holes in an otherwise unblemished but rapidly darkening sky. It was a nice evening for a walk, she told herself, although recently the mile and a half, mostly uphill, had proved to be almost too much even for her. She gritted her teeth, ignored the ache in her knees and the uncomfortable feeling in her chest and started up the rise. She was damned if she was going to give way as her mother had, and spend much of the last years of her life in a bath chair. She imagined sitting up there behind the horses, the coachman in his fine uniform, the people looking up admiringly as Miss Willmott was driven to her estate and the finest private garden in England.

The few shops and the street lights were soon left behind, replaced by houses occupied by people of little consequence to her, the light from their windows supplementing the glimmer from the thin moon just now appearing over the rooftops. She wondered how many of them had been employed by her over the years, or at least owed part of their income to her presence in Great Warley. Her garden had been graced by many in high places, including royalty, and she wasn't short of telling people that; but what gave her even greater satisfaction were the visits from the more discerning groups. The Essex Field Club still came from time to time and its members were impressed by her sadly diminishing plant collection, but aficionados from abroad were rarely seen now.

How she yearned for those carefree days with her sister Rose in Aix les Bains, taking the cure. She'd suffered from rheumatism that long ago, forty-four years to be precise, but it hadn't stopped her then and it wasn't going to stop her now. Alright, she and Rose had been well looked after by Lady Whalley and Dr Bracket… strange that, she thought, she could remember names from the distant past but had trouble remembering yesterday; or even this morning. Then she had bought the villa in Tresserve. Oh, what a lovely time they had had, improving the building and developing the garden; constructing an alpine garden second only to the one at Warley; seven hundred rose plants in a rose garden, with three hundred different roses. Then the fire; that had been really hard, but she'd even got over that. What had gone wrong? Why had she sold it? The war, that was it, the war had ruined everything.

She was alone now, as she preferred to be. Apart from, she suddenly realised, the faint sound of footsteps some distance behind.

Cemetery Road appeared on the right and she stared straight ahead as she passed by, ignoring the headstones at the far end behind the gate as they watched silently and reproachfully while she continued on her journey. Rosina Maurer, her faithful alpine gardener Jacob Maurer's first wife, was buried there, she knew. She was aware also that he could not afford a headstone for her and had buried his wife in an unmarked grave. She'd heard that he had planted a juniper tree to indicate the spot, and that some were wondering why she had not paid for something better. But why should she have done? Could he not have managed his finances more efficiently and put something aside for such an emergency? He had worked for her since the age of nineteen, so had had plenty of time to do so. Was it her fault that he had fathered nine children and spent all his wages, thirty-five shillings a week no less, on keeping them? She walked on.

She allowed a modicum of concern to register when she was uncomfortably passing the huge Victorian Gothic edifice of Brentwood Mental Hospital and realised that the footsteps, once some way behind, were closer now.

On one occasion she'd had a similar experience and surreptitiously dropped the bag containing her tiara into the bushes, to be retrieved the following morning, but this day she had no such riches to worry about. The local vagabonds would not know her well-kept secret though, and would welcome the chance to snatch the bag she carried.

It could be one of the patients who had escaped. Perhaps he did not want to steal, just to kill or to maim in some violent fashion; or even – no, not that, not to someone of her age, surely? He would be waiting for a suitable place in which to carry out his dastardly attack. Her heart beat a little faster. She was in no condition to run, but by God she'd leave her mark on him before he was finished.

She heard a car coming in the distance and a little Austin chugged past, making heavy weather of the hill but nevertheless doing far better than she was. She considered waving to the driver for assistance but could not bring herself to do so, and he was gone.

The road levelled out now and as she passed the Protestant Christ Church on her left and the Holy Cross and All Saints Catholic church on her right, she quickened her pace a little. They were both deserted and their tree-lined paths were no refuge, providing only cover for anyone with evil intentions. Her parents had paid for the All Saints altar, the reredos, the stained glass windows above, and later the porch. She had herself paid for furnishing the Lady Chapel and taken charge of the choir; her sister Rose had married Robert Berkeley there. But a fat lot of good any of that would do her if she were to be molested now.

She was sure the footsteps behind had speeded up. Damn Robinson, why had he not insisted on meeting her? Warley Barracks was looming on the left at the crossroads and the Horse and Groom public house on the right, so her assailant – for that is what she now considered him to be – would have to act soon. She quickened her own steps so that her screams might be heard. Then she saw a figure coming towards her from the front; his accomplice no doubt. Her heart sank, as even she could see that now there was no escape.

The man, for now she could see that's what he was, drew closer and she allowed herself a faint hope for a good outcome. Even in the dim light she could see this was no scoundrel, but a person she knew instinctively she could trust; a man with honest eyes, upright in stature, a faint smile to his lips; someone who although not young was nevertheless strong enough to take care of himself, but someone who would not strike the first blow. And he had a dog. A great big lolloping dog, not one of those vicious fighting dogs but nevertheless one that looked well able to protect its master if the need arose. Adorned as he was, simply, with no ornamentation at all, she had little clue to his background, but felt safe in his presence. He stopped as he drew near.

'Good evening,' he said. 'I think you could do with some help. May I take your bag?'

She stopped and the footsteps from behind got louder and then a figure slouched passed and she shuddered. Now there was a mean face if ever there was one, just visible under the cap pulled down over his dark eyebrows, and a red and black kerchief tied round his neck. A low growl came from the dog, all the more menacing because it was only just audible.

She knew that she had had a narrow escape this time. Never again would she make this journey alone.

Looking at her saviour as he stroked the hound's head, she was puzzled at his open self-assurance. Not with the way he ignored the other man, the dog would be enough for that, but with her. Most people were very cautious about approaching her. 'Do I know you?' she asked.

He smiled. 'No, I just thought you might do with some assistance.'

'I am very grateful,' Ellen Willmott said, and indeed she was. 'I should be able to make my way satisfactorily now though.'

'I should feel better if you would allow me to accompany you until you are safely home.' It wasn't a request.

She looked along the road where the dark figure had disappeared. 'I would welcome your company, but I fear I am putting you to some inconvenience.'

'Not at all,' he said. 'I was just walking Rufus. Although I fancy he would rather be curled up on his sofa just now.'

She found herself wondering who he was, where he lived, what he did for a living, and indeed why he had stopped to help her, but he was silent as he accompanied her, his eyes probing the darkness. Only once did he speak, and that was when the thin moon was hidden by trees and he stopped to look at the magnificence of the Milky Way, stretched across the sky as if a celestial artist had whitewashed the heavens with a sweep of his brush.

'It's beautiful, isn't it?' he commented. 'All those stars, all those planets, just like ours.' Then, 'Sorry, you need to get home.'

'No,' she said. 'It is so easy to take such things for granted. To look, but not to see.' Then, with a lilt in her voice, 'But the daffodils in my meadow would give them a run for their money!'

They moved on, but she suddenly realised how lonely she had been.

Once they had passed Headley Common they both breathed easier and soon the gate to North Lodge, one of the two entrances to Warley Place, appeared.

'I shall be safe from here,' she said. 'I am much obliged.'

'I don't wish to intrude,' he said, 'but that man may resent his plans being thwarted. He could easily be waiting in the bushes in your drive. May I accompany you to your house? Then I will continue out past South Lodge if I may.'

She hesitated, but knew he was right. The drive was quite long and certainly contained many places where someone could hide, pounce and then disappear.

'Very well, that is most kind.'

They moved on, passing the lodge.

'Do you know my garden then? That the drive continues to South Lodge?'

'I have never been inside, but have seen it from the road and have heard it spoken of. A remarkable achievement, I believe; and very beautiful.'

They reached the coach turning circle and the front door to Warley Place itself.

'I don't know your name,' she said.

'Edward Saxon.'

'Well, Edward Saxon, it would be my pleasure to show you my garden in the daylight at our mutual convenience, if you wish. Meanwhile I thank you and bid you a very good night.'

'It has been my pleasure Miss Willmott,' he said, turning and continuing down the carriage drive. After a few yards Rufus turned his head to look at her, and she found herself smiling and waving at him, before remembering who she was and quickly putting her arm to her side.

She was looking thoughtfully after this enigmatic figure as he disappeared into the darkness, dog ambling along beside him, and wondering at his timely appearance, when the front door opened and the tall figure of her butler stood there, stepping aside to allow her to make her way in to the safety of her house. Robinson glanced down the drive hearing the footsteps crunching on the gravel and wondered who had been with his mistress, but knew better than to ask. He was just glad she was home, so that he could make his way to his own bed.

2

Clearing South Pond
March 2013

'All right,' said David as the volunteers gathered round on a cold but thankfully dry Monday morning. 'Today we're going to clear round the edge of South Pond.'

There was a collective groan. The carriage drive used to be the main road to Brentwood, and South Pond used to be a water supply for Great Warley in medieval times. The pond continued as a watering hole for horses until the by-pass was constructed and the pond became part of the estate. Plants growing round its perimeter included reeds, yellow flags and marsh marigolds, while moorhens and mallards nested there. Firecrests, goldcrests and many other birds could be seen from a hide constructed on the far side.

David, of slim but muscular build, was the warden, responsible for all the work that was carried out at Warley Place. He had taken over from Frank who had handed over the reins to his much younger colleague – younger, indeed, than most of those working for him. A volunteer like the rest of them, his sense of humour was essential in dealing with the ribald comments directed at him. He was also adept at maintaining, repairing and adapting the equipment used on the reserve.

'Oh dear, and I've forgotten my wellington boots,' said Gordon, stroking his greying beard, a smile twitching at the corners of his mouth, knowing quite well what was coming next. He had been volunteering there for fifteen years or so and they were well used to his rather dry and sometimes hard to fathom sense of humour.

'Don't you worry,' replied David, 'We've got a nice pair of waders hanging up in the shed, just your size.'

'And of what relevance is it that the shed is just my size?' asked Gordon.

'And what about you Ken, fancy joining him?' suggested David, ignoring Gordon's good-humoured pedantry in his usual fashion.

Ken, a much younger man, was fortunate to be running a small specialist plant nursery and able to join the volunteers on a Monday morning. He had been a volunteer for ten years or so and Warley Place was where he had met Elsie, now his wife, two years ago, marrying her after just a few months. Being open over weekends, the nursery was shut on Mondays leaving Ken time to continue volunteering at Warley Place. From time to time Elsie was able to join him, much to the pleasure not only of Ken but the rest of the volunteers also.

'That's fine,' he said.

The others breathed sighs of relief, for there were only two pairs of waders. Their reprieve proved to be short-lived however when David continued.

'And someone will be joining me in the boat.'

'But we might fall in and drown,' said Norman. 'We'd need the proper equipment. Have you done a Health and Safety assessment?'

Norman was a very old hand in both senses of the word and well versed in the Health and Safety regulations. Although comments about the subject flew thick and fast, they all knew how important it was and how many hazards there were at Warley Place.

'Yes, I've done a Health and Safety Assessment. The equipment is in the boat.'

'We don't have a boat,' said Gordon hopefully.

'We do now,' replied David. 'I borrowed one from Hanningfield and brought it on my trailer. Right, Donald, fancy joining me?'

'As long as I get to sit at the captain's table for lunch.'

'The rest of you will be carting the dirty wet smelly weed-ridden slimy sludge to the waste ground behind the car park.'

He grinned. They all groaned. Some of them had done this sort of thing before, when de-sludging the reservoirs, and knew full well how filthy they would be before the morning was over.

'You can come out from behind the tree, Peter,' continued David loudly, 'and bring Martin, he's hiding in his car.'

'OK if I take some photographs?' asked Robert, another of the more mature (no-one used the word 'elderly') volunteers. 'It will be worth recording.' He had a camera bag containing a Canon SLR camera, several lenses, and other bits and pieces a mystery to most of the volunteers. He hoisted it out of his car and slung it over his shoulder, trying hard not to show how heavy he now found it.

What was once a beautiful garden had become a wilderness after Ellen Willmott's death. Then in 1977, after forty-three years of deterioration, Essex Wildlife Trust took on the management of what became a nature reserve, but managing it in a way that visitors could imagine what it was like in its previous owner's day.

One of the main features had been the Alpine Garden, comprising a man-made gorge with a stream draining into South Pond. A number of years ago a mechanical digger was brought in to dredge the pond but the sedges and rushes had encroached again so needed to be cut back considerably, while leaving enough for wildlife habitat – mostly moorhens and sometimes ducks.

The stream had long since dried up. In fact, no-one was certain where the water had come from and why South Pond had not overflowed. One theory was that it was pumped back up to the upper pond from where the stream originated, topped up from the mains to cater for evaporation and other losses, but no trace of a pump had ever been found and what archives there were made no reference to any. Since there was no electrical supply to the site in those days, it would have had to be powered in some other way, so the use of a pump also seemed doubtful.

Robert had taken over the task of keeping records of what was happening and to catalogue archives in general as they became available. Since dredging the pond was something that did not happen often, it was useful to have a photographic as well as a written record. It was also a good way of avoiding the heaviest or dirtiest jobs!

'That's fine Robert,' said David, 'but if you make any money out of a picture of me falling in then I want half!'

'Right everyone, there are a couple of cromes in the shed, also some rakes to get the rushes out of the water, then forks to hoist it on to wheelbarrows to take it away. If anyone needs disposable overalls they are on the shelf.'

'What's a crome?' asked Robert.

'It's a wicked looking hook on the end of a long pole, meant for just this sort of job. It can also be used to retrieve volunteers who wander off.'

Four of them walked up the slope to the store and loaded three wheelbarrows with tools; as the others went back to the pond Robert quickly took 'before' shots, firstly from the carriage drive and then, carefully making his way round the pond, from the other side.

David handed a life preserver to Donald and put his own on, before the two of them pushed the aluminium boat into the water; he looked at them all, a dozen volunteers, putting on waders, wheeling wheelbarrows to the pond's edge and choosing tools, and laughing with each other despite knowing what state they were going to be in before long. All with so very different backgrounds and all who had ended up together for a variety of reasons, or because of chance encounters of one sort or another and who melded into a team any manager would give his eye teeth for.

'Oh, and Gordon,' David called out. Gordon had donned the waders and was standing holding a crome staring at all the vegetation growing thickly round the complete perimeter of the pond. He looked up at the sound of David's voice.

'Could you try to get rid of the bamboo in front of the Royal Fern,' David asked him, pointing to the north side of the water.

'The what?' shouted Gordon.

'In the middle there.' He pointed to a stump half in and half out of the pond behind a clump of bamboo.

'That? There's nothing royal about that! It's just a half dead fern.'

'Yes, but soon it will grow again and it will look very royal indeed. Just be careful, it's quite rare in Essex.'

David watched for a moment and then he and Donald got in the boat with their rakes and pushed it through the reeds away from the shore.

The Royal Fern, or *Osmunda regalis*, used to be quite

common but became less so when areas were drained for agriculture. In addition the roots were used as part of a growing medium for orchids so, in Essex at least, it had become an unusual sight and was well looked after at Warley Place.

The surface of the water, which had previously been like a millpond, was now criss-crossed with miniature waves from volunteers splashing in the slippery shallows to uproot the rushes, and dragging their prizes to the banks. Others, with forks, heaved their oozing loads on to wheelbarrows, where still more willing men wheeled them dripping a trail of mud to the car park, behind which was a useful low patch of waste ground.

David kept a close eye on Gordon and Ken in their waders, the water rising above their knees. A slip on the muddy bottom might seem very funny, but if either of them swallowed any of the water it could be a hospital visit for them. Working in stagnant water was normally avoided because of the health risk, particularly Weil's Disease, but this was a job that had been put off until it was now essential. There were certainly rats about so the water was equally certainly contaminated with their urine. Volunteers were protected with rubber gloves and David had made sure no-one with open cuts was involved, so he felt the risks were manageable.

Happy that things were as safe as they could be, he and Donald started pulling up the rushes the rest of the volunteers could not reach and heaving them into the boat, then taking them to the bank to be unloaded.

Although the lady volunteers were every bit as hard working as the men, they were obviously not as physically strong, so on occasions such as this they worked elsewhere – today, in the walled garden, where they were doing their best to remove the abundant weeds that threatened to choke the flowers that were once Ellen Willmott's pride and joy. Robert paid them a brief visit, then stuck a macro lens on his camera and wandered off to search for photogenic insects.

About an hour later he returned and carefully made his way round the slippery bank, standing on the flat milestones which the Backhouse men, who constructed the gorge, had laid there as a sort of landing stage. He clicked away on his camera for a few minutes, oblivious to ribald comments from his friends. Then, looking at his watch and seeing that there were fifteen minutes to go before tea break, he walked further round to where the little stream that ran through the gorge discharged into the pond. Looking up towards the bridge over the deepest section he saw, as he had often done before, the huge boulders that lined the steep slopes and among which flowers once grew that were acclaimed by all who saw them. Now there were none of Ellen Willmott's original flowers left, although the purple of the purple toothwort, *Lathrea clandestina*, could be seen in the gorge and on the upper slopes at this time of the year.

He crossed the valley and looked with admiration at the remains of the filmy-fern cave. There appeared to have been a small tributary from the main stream, and over it had been built a cave out of rocks. Those forming the sides were mostly still in place, as were those forming archways at the front and rear of the cave – although the very heavy-looking keystones looked as though they could fall at any moment. An old wooden door leaned on one of the rocks, and pieces of glass over half an inch thick that used to form the roof could still be seen. Rusty glazing bars spanned the open roof.

No trace of the ferns that were grown in there had been found, but he imagined Ellen Willmott and Jacob Maurer ducking slightly and walking in to tend to their valuable charges. Fitting a wide-angle lens, minding the rabbit holes and mossy rocks, he made his way up to the doorway. Bending down, he took a shot of the view and quickly crouched and walked through to the other end, then turned and took a picture from that direction.

He reminded himself, under his breath, that the corroded glazing bars could split his scalp if he stood up, and at a slow crouching walk, returned the way he had come. He had a feeling that David would have frowned upon him doing that and would, sensibly, have insisted at least on him wearing a hard hat.

There were boulders all round, and it was on one of them that he sat while he put his camera into its bag. He looked away from the pond towards the bridge, and wondered how on earth the contractor had managed to form the steep slopes with such heavy rocks and few mechanical aids. He tried to imagine what it was like there, how Ellen Willmott managed to make her way up and down the slopes and what Jacob Maurer thought of her interfering. It seemed that the harder he tried to visualise it the less he succeeded but sometimes, when he was just relaxing and enjoying the peace and tranquillity, the feeling that she was still there was real enough for him to look round, half expecting to see her. This was one of those occasions, and the slight breeze even allowed the trees to whisper to him that all was well now that this magical garden was being cared for.

His reverie was broken by the sound of the volunteers putting tools down and a couple of them pulling the boat up the bank so that David and Donald could disembark and have a well-earned tea break with the rest. He picked his camera bag up, grunted a little at the weight, then looked again at the rocky slopes. How on earth did Ellen Willmott manage to cart a heavy tripod, full plate camera, spare plates, probably light meter, notebooks and other paraphernalia up and down these slopes – or anywhere else for that matter. Audrey le Lièvre, in her biography of Ellen Willmott, noted that it was carried by the footman, William. Robert felt sorry for him – goodness knows what she would say if he slipped and dropped the camera! She later used a much smaller film camera, but the quality of the photographs would not have been as good as with the large glass plates. And to think she processed her pictures herself, in her own darkroom! No digital technology for her.

The others all made their way up the drive to the conservatory, discarding gloves but still leaving a trail of watery mud and vegetation, as if a giant snail had slithered along the path. He took a short cut across the Pleasaunce, wondering at what it must have looked like when croquet and tennis were played just below the dwarf wall, in an area now dotted with trees, mounds and rabbit holes.

A series of humorous pointed comments were made by the female volunteers who had been working in the walled garden. The comments mostly revolved round the aroma that now pervaded the room, despite the large openings in the walls and the lack of a roof, but also the condition of their footwear and the smudges on their faces. They petered out when Gordon, who was in a particularly filthy state, promised to give Anne a good hug when tea break was over.

After the usual twenty minutes or so they all made their somewhat slower way back to the pond to finish the job they had started. Fortunately they had broken the back of it and made good enough progress to finish the clearance just in time for lunch. Most of them eased their weary bones back to the conservatory to collect their bags before heading for the car park and home for a welcome shower.

After the wheelbarrows and tools were taken back to the store Gordon and Robert made their way back to the conservatory to eat their lunch with David and to discuss what needed to be done to ensure the reserve was safe and presentable for the public. Gordon had found a hand rail needing attention on the path down to the North Hide; some of the path markers were rotten and should be replaced; otherwise the next major item would be checking the boundary fences for when the cattle were let into the reserve to get the grass down.

'Funny, isn't it,' said Gordon, 'the way this place gets to you. When I retired I thought I'd play golf, maybe potter in the garden, maybe do a bit of walking – but not join Essex Wildlife Trust and …….. Robert, are you listening?'

'Yes,' said Robert, sliding his camera out of his bag. 'Sort of. Look, a *Pyrochroa coccinea*. Isn't it lovely.'

'A what?'

Robert sighed noisily and rolled his eyes, changing his lens to a much bigger one. 'A cardinal beetle to you, I suppose.'

'Why do you need a telephoto lens when it's that close?'

'It's not a telephoto, it's a macro lens. I use it mostly for insects.'

'How do you know it's a, um, a whatsit?'

'Has it occurred to you that I might be an expert entomologist?'

'Very briefly,' laughed Gordon. 'Come on, is it really one? Or did you make it up?'

'Oh, all right,' confessed Robert. 'I saw one last week and looked it up in my book and remembered the name. At least, I think I remembered the name; and I think it was the same as that one.'

He slid the camera back into its recess in his bag.

'What were you saying?'

'It doesn't matter,' moaned Gordon sorrowfully. 'I know I'm beaten when an insect gets more attention than I do.'

'Don't you two ever tire of winding each other up?' grinned David.

'Not really,' they both said.

'I was listening, actually,' said Robert. 'Yes, it does get to you. I was just out for a drive with Louise and saw the gate open. It was an open weekend, so we went in and I got chatting…'

'As you are wont to do,' commented David.

'Well, yes,' admitted Robert. 'Anyway, I just knew straight away that it's where I wanted to spend some time. Doing a worthwhile job, keeping myself fit, meeting interesting people, what's not to like? What about you, Gordon?'

'I heard about it from a neighbour, so came to see what it was about and, same as you, I liked the people and the work. But also – and I know it sounds silly – I just get a strange feeling sometimes that we're being watched.'

'By Health and Safety inspectors?' suggested David.

'Yes, them too!'

'I know what you mean,' said Robert. 'The characters who worked here – the gardeners, Jacob Maurer, Ellen Willmott herself, they are all still here.'

26

'If they are, I hope they appreciate what we're doing,' said David.

'And that they feel embarrassed about the Japanese knotweed, Himalayan balsam, giant hogweed, to name but a few,' grinned Gordon.

They finished their food in silence, until eventually they followed the others and made their way out of the gate to home for a much-needed change of clothing and shower.

3

The Saxon Family
June 1934

Edward Saxon looked up from his favourite book, the Rancocas edition of the 18th century Quaker John Woolman's Journal, his forehead creased, eyes wide, and his mouth opening and shutting as he shook his head.

'No Howard, please, no.' The words came eventually.

'I must, father. I know how you think about war and this is the best way to stop it. That new German chancellor, Hitler, is a megalomaniac. He wants to take over Europe, us with it, and he will if he sees any sign of weakness.'

'But no-one wins a war. We all lose.'

'We'll lose a damn sight more if we don't defend our principles,' Howard said heatedly.

'Howard!'

'Sorry father, it's just that I feel very strongly about it.' He squeezed himself into the end of the well-worn sofa not occupied by Rufus, their big hound of doubtful provenance. 'The Versailles Treaty is dead, everyone knows that. The Germans have been allowed to just walk away from it. I agree we should talk but we must have strength to back up what we say. That's why I want to go. I want to enlist with the RAF. I want to fly and protect the country I love.'

'Versailles crippled Germany,' said his father. 'They simply can't afford the reparations that have been demanded. It's not surprising they are rebelling. Unemployment has gone sky high in the last few years. It's just the sort of atmosphere in which people like this Hitler fellow thrive, I know that. But I couldn't bear to lose you too.'

Howard was quiet for a moment. His dear mother had died in the 1918 flu epidemic, as had so many others. He had been four years old at the time and could just about remember her warm arms round him when he had hurt himself, and her soft voice when putting him to bed. Sixteen years later he still missed her.

'If we stand firm he won't invade us. The English Channel will help, and anyway we have too much in common with the German people for them to stand for it.'

'I don't think personal connections or relations with the Royal Family are going to help much,' his father replied. 'And be that as it may, would our government stand aside while he conquers the rest of Europe?'

'So you think a war is inevitable?'

'Didn't Herodotus say "No-one is fool enough to choose war instead of peace – in peace sons bury their fathers, but in war fathers bury their sons"?' sighed Edward. 'But yes, it will happen. Not next year, nor the year after, but not that far ahead. Hitler already has his eyes on Austria and the parts of Czechoslovakia closest to Germany. He'll move in there first, and the consequences horrify me.'

'I know our family has a long Quaker tradition,' said Howard, more quietly now, stroking Rufus' head as it stirred on his lap. 'But you did your bit in the last war, didn't you?'

'That was different,' said Edward. 'The Friends Ambulance Unit was formed to help the wounded of both sides, to save lives, not to kill and maim.'

'But didn't many of your fellow Quakers feel that in doing so you released others to fight?'

'They did,' sighed Edward. 'But we treated not only soldiers, but also the local civilians in France who suffered terribly. Although the unit was set up initially by Friends, outside the strictures of their faith, many non-Quakers joined too.

'But joining the FAU did nothing to stop the war. It had already started. By joining the Royal Air Force I shall help to prevent such a conflict and will hopefully never have to fight.'

'You can use all the logic in the world,' said Edward, glancing down at his book. 'Some of us are convinced that violence is wrong; always.'

'Convinced by what? The world has changed, father. In George Fox's day people could kill one man at a time, usually face to face or at worst with a musket. Now with machine guns, and bombs, and aeroplanes, who knows how many will die. It's no use telling a bitter enemy that violence is wrong. He has to know he cannot win. Hasn't Hitler already brought in a law banning Jews from doing any sort of civil service work, including teaching? And aren't Jewish shops already being vandalised and looted?'

'Our principles cannot be dismissed that easily, but I admit, standing by while others are being so persecuted is difficult to justify.'

'What about William Penn and his principles? He founded Pennsylvania based on Quaker principles. What happened? The immigrants didn't share those principles so pretty soon it was no longer a Quaker province. It was an experiment that failed.'

'The democratic principles that he devised were used as a basis for the United States Constitution, so he did not fail. He also purchased land from the American Indians rather than just commandeering it as many others did, and honoured agreements made with them, which was unusual. But it is true that his wishes for the long-term management of what became Pennsylvania did not bear fruit. I'm afraid my knowledge of this very complicated situation is insufficient to do it justice, but I do take your point.'

'Well to simplify it, if someone had attacked me while I was a baby, or mother, and force was the only way to prevent it, what would you have done?'

'I know, the usual argument, and I have to admit it's one that I cannot answer. Quakers in the old days would all have said no, violence would still have been wrong. Many paid for it with their lives. I don't think I could have been that strong – certainly not strong enough to pay for it with someone else's life.'

'Can I go with your blessing?'

'You must do as you think right. I understand why you would want to do this thing. But I think you are wrong and I have failed in not convincing you that you are wrong.'

'I don't want to hurt you father. I do hope it doesn't cause you too much embarrassment with Friends.'

'They will understand. Not long ago it would have been unheard of, but a certain ambivalence is creeping in about the use of force in a just cause, especially with our younger members. I think if we do all we can to deal with the causes of violence, each in our own way, then perhaps that will have to be enough. You have chosen a path I would not have chosen, but who am I to say which of us is right?'

'I shall be living away from home for most of the time,' said Howard anxiously. 'I worry about you being lonely here on your own.'

'Friends will no doubt keep an eye on me, whether or not I attend Meetings.'

'Why do Quakers call each other Friends?'

'It's just a convenient term to denote people close to you. Jesus used the term, according to John – chapter 15 as I recall. It does cause a little confusion at times, I must admit, but it doesn't really matter.'

He thought for a moment.

'Anyway, even apart from Friends I won't be on my own, I have my work, and in the evenings Rufus and my books.'

The family dog opened an eye at the sound of his name, then seeing nothing of any great interest shut it again, stretched and went back to sleep.

'But you are bored with your work. The company will run itself; you've often said so.'

Edward nodded. Many years before he had started a small company designing and installing heating and plumbing systems, but having proved to be an excellent judge of men's character and capability, and taken them on in key positions, he found himself with little to do other than keep an unnecessary overall eye on things. The income was not enough to make him rich, but sufficient for his needs.

'I may take a short break,' he said. 'Do something completely different for a while, something useful, and to get another perspective on life. I have something in mind.'

'What is that then?'

'I'll let you know later. It may come to nothing.'

'Something to do with Friends?'

'No. Quakerism is an important part of my life and has given me support more times than I can remember. But when the time comes and I am standing in front of my God I wish to be able to answer that I have done things because I thought they were the right things to have done, not because others thought so or I read it in a book. I want to leave the world in a better state than when I entered it, but sometimes the right path is not so easy to find. I want to clear my head so that I can consider these matters.'

And perhaps, he thought, he could also consider the biggest question of all – whether there was indeed a God, or at any rate one that a mere human being could possibly envisage.

'So you don't want to be another Tomlinson!' commented Howard.

'No, certainly not,' laughed his father.

He wasn't a great lover of poetry, but Rudyard Kipling's poem was a favourite. Written many years earlier, it was the story of a man who went to Heaven but was not allowed in because he hadn't really done anything to improve man's lot on earth. He went to Hell but the devil wouldn't let him in there either, because he hadn't been bad enough to waste good coal on.

'Well father, I look forward to hearing your conclusions and discussing them with you, if you will allow me that privilege.'

'I too look forward to it.'

But a great sadness overtook him at that point and he closed his eyes so that his son could not see the water start to gather.

'You want to fly then?' he said eventually.

'Yes father. It must be a wonderful feeling to be up there, the wind whistling past as you dive down at more than two hundred miles an hour, or climb up and see the clouds from above and to fly through them or round them; to loop the loop, or roll and turn at the movement of the stick and the pedals.'

'Didn't a young pilot lose his legs doing that?'

'Oh, yes, Douglas Bader. But he was doing a roll too low down and trying to show off I believe. I wouldn't do that.'

A wry smile was the only answer from Edward.

'I might even fly one of the new Hawker Furys,' continued Howard. 'They can go over 200 miles an hour straight and level, much faster in a dive. They are beautiful. And they can reach nearly thirty thousand feet high, that's as high as Mount Everest.'

'And every bit as cold I expect.'

'So I am told; you have to wear the right clothes and have oxygen to breathe.'

'Being fighters, presumably they have guns?'

'Well, yes, two Vickers machine guns.'

'I wonder what they would do to a man if he got in their way?'

Howard was silent for a moment.

'But as I said before, if we are able to defend ourselves then we won't need to shoot anyone. The knowledge that we could would be enough.'

'Of course, they might put you in a bomber,' said Edward. 'One of those Handley Page things, a Heyford isn't it?'

'How did you know that?' asked Howard.

'Just because I don't like violence it doesn't mean

I don't keep up with the news. It carries over a ton of bombs I believe. Could you really bring yourself to drop those on people?'

'If they were at war with us, and soldiers, yes, I suppose so.'

'And from high in the sky would you be able to tell they were soldiers? Could you drop the bombs accurately enough to know you would hit them and not civilians nearby? Could you blow up human beings, soldiers or not?'

'I know what you are trying to do father, but I said before, I want to stop it ever getting to that stage.'

Edward sighed.

'I can only repeat, I do not agree with what you are about to do, but if you have seriously considered all these matters and really think that it is the right thing to do then you must do it. What happens next?'

'I'll visit the recruiting office in the morning and ask them. I believe it all happens quite quickly after that.'

Edward picked up his book again but could not read the blurred words.

Howard saw the book upside down in his father's hands and felt a lump come to his throat.

4

An Open Weekend
April 2013

'The last one then,' said Donald as he opened the tailgate of his car and sat down to put his boots on.

'The last weekend, yes. I'll be glad to be able take it easy after tomorrow,' said Gordon, already booted but putting his gloves on.

Although the general public were allowed in at any time unaccompanied, on weekends for a couple of months each year the reserve was manned by Essex Wildlife Trust volunteers, who were on hand to tell visitors about the history of Ellen Willmott and her garden, and to sell small items to make money for maintenance and improvement purposes. This involved erecting a gazebo and preparing the sale items in advance of the public's arrival, and then being on hand to deal with their needs. On one day a guided tour was also provided for a modest additional donation.

A squeaking wheelbarrow came round the corner of a three metre high hedge, pushed by Robert.

'Something wrong there,' said Gordon. 'We could hear squeak....... squeak....... squeak...' from a hundred yards away.

'I know,' said Robert. 'It needs to be oiled.'

'No, it's not that,' said Gordon. 'It should have been going 'squeaksqueaksqueak'. You obviously weren't walking fast enough.'

'I hadn't realised you were old enough to remember that joke,' said Robert. 'Do you want any help leaning on that car?'

Daphne, also a long-standing volunteer, followed them as they walked to the entrance, carrying a bag.

It was the work of a moment to lift the gazebo off the wheelbarrow and after a few minutes heaving and grunting they left it standing waiting for its sides to be added. These provided excellent protection from the wind and, sometimes, the rain, which would otherwise have ruined the sale items, and also very handy for those sitting at the large wooden picnic table that was now being shifted into position.

Two smaller collapsible tables were erected and were soon covered in books, cards, arts and crafts items and collection tins. Bird boxes and feeding poles were hung on hooks, notices placed at the gate and a float provided for the collection box. Although entry was free, a donation for the upkeep was invited by means of notices at the entrance.

'OK, if that's all I'll be off now,' said Robert, who helped to get things ready on each weekend throughout these two months. 'I'll see you tomorrow Daphne.'

'Me too,' said Donald. 'I'm on duty this afternoon and on Sunday so Monday will be three days in a row for me.'

'I'll just take a quick stroll, Daphne,' said Gordon. 'I'll be back before they start rolling in.'

'No hurry,' said Daphne. 'Martin, Beryl and Peter will be here later. Peter can man the gate, Martin can see to the car parking and Beryl and I can look after things here. Don't forget you have a tour this morning, unless you want me to take it?'

'I forgot that,' groaned Gordon. 'I wonder if there will

be the usual know-it-all, or someone who lags behind or someone who speeds on ahead; or all of those.'

'There might be,' agreed Daphne. 'I can do it if you prefer.'

'No, I just like complaining,' said Gordon grinning. 'Actually I don't mind taking people round whatever they are like, it makes the time pass more quickly. And in fact most of them are brilliant, especially if they laugh at my jokes!'

'I'd forgotten your guided tour,' said Robert. 'I'll hang on for a bit in case it's very busy.'

'Me too,' said Donald. 'I tell you what, Robert, we could join Gordon's tour and ask awkward questions.'

'You dare!' threatened Gordon.

He wandered up the drive, revelling in the peace that would shortly be shattered; that was the plan, anyway. The more people, the more money for the reserve. Although actually, he realised, his main concern was to satisfy visitors' interest in the history and botanical content, not to raise money, however important that might be.

One of the good things about Warley Place was that the great majority of the visitors were so good natured, interested and appreciative of the peace and tranquillity the reserve offered. Occasionally it was obvious that a husband or wife had been dragged along by a spouse and would rather be at home watching the television, but that was rare. And vandalism, too, was almost unheard of and litter mostly cleared and taken home rather than dropped.

He turned off at the carriage turning circle and made his way past the headache tree to the walled garden to sit, for a moment, on one of the benches.

The large-leafed magnolia, *Magnolia obovata*, was really showing its age and he wondered how much longer it could survive. Fortunately, a seedling from this very tree, propagated by one of the volunteers, was growing very well and in a few years' time would hopefully produce its first flower. They were both dwarfed by the huge *Ginkgo biloba*, which produced such brilliant yellow leaves in the autumn. Its height had not been measured accurately but it was very tall indeed, and its girth of well over two and a half metres meant it must be one of the largest in England, if not further.

He looked at the south wall, the one re-pointed those few years ago in which Donald had found the mysterious package. If he hadn't told Donald about Warley Place it would probably have still been there now. Life's twists and turns were fascinating – one never knew what tomorrow might bring and where it might lead.

The garden was smothered in colour, mostly the yellow of the daffodils but also many other plants, the names of which he was always embarrassed not to be able to remember, despite having been told many times.

When here on his own he often imagined Ellen Willmott walking round, bending down here, reaching up there, snipping at this, admiring that. And Jacob Maurer too, mostly down by the Alpine Garden scrambling up and down the rocks looking after his precious plants. At times they both seemed so very real.

He glanced at his watch; whoops, visitors would be arriving soon, best be going. He rose to his feet and, making for the exit to the garden, he stopped and looked at some wild daffodils, *Narcissus pseudonarcissus*, right in the corner. He smiled to himself.

After a quick look at the greenhouses behind the north wall, he hurried back to the gate and found Peter ushering the first vehicles into their places in the car park. Sunday was always the busier of the two days, but with the weather as nice as it was this Saturday would be busier than most.

An hour later the car park was half full and a small group of people were gathering by the gazebo waiting for the ten-thirty tour. He looked at them before approaching. All ten wearing sensible footwear; some ageing but mobile; mostly looking happy – but, oh dear, one he knew instinctively would be awkward. A middle-aged man looking bored as his wife spoke to him. He was not tall, of similar size to her, dark haired and had darkish hair and a moustache.

Gordon went up to them.

'Hello everyone,' he said loudly, 'My name is Gordon and I'll be taking you round today.'

Smiles and attention from all of them – except Adolph.

'Just a few words about health and safety.'

Adolph looked wearily at a passing cloud.

'Please keep to the paths. There are rabbit holes and other hazards and you could easily break your ankle. If you want to get closer to something to take a photograph, just ask and take care.'

The cloud had gone and Adolph was inspecting his fingernails.

'There are some barbed wire fences and steps, and it's probably best not to lean on the fences as they may not be quite strong enough.'

'Right, we will now go along what used to be the main road to Brentwood until 1866, when the by-pass was built.'

'And the road from Brentwood,' said Adolph.

'Thank you for pointing that out,' said Gordon, 'but it was the road to Brentwood from here.'

Adolph's wife - Teresa, Gordon decided that was her name, for being good enough to stay with him - gave her husband one of those looks; a look that he totally ignored.

Gordon wondered if he had read anything about Warley Place and thought he'd find out.

'Before we go on,' he said, 'you may have noticed the white cottage by the gate.'

'Jacob Maurer's cottage,' said Adolph.

Teresa shut her eyes for a moment.

'Yes, Jacob Maurer's cottage.'

'It's a shame it's not been very well maintained.'

'Yes,' agreed Gordon. 'Unfortunately it's not part of the reserve so there's not much we can do about it.'

Gordon told them about Jacob's vital role as Ellen Willmott's alpine gardener, coming to Warley Place at nineteen years of age and staying for forty years. The area alongside the cottage, now part of the Thatchers' and Warley Place car parks, used to be a working area, with greenhouses and nursery beds, for Jacob's use in propagating Alpine plants.

'Then, after Ellen Willmott's death, instead of inheriting the cottage he was forced to leave and went to stay with his son John in Gidea Park.'

'No,' said Adolph triumphantly, 'Billericay.'

'Gidea Park,' repeated Gordon.

'It says Billericay in Audrey le Lievre's book,' said Adolph.

'John did not move to Billericay until after his father's death,' said Gordon. 'It was an easy mistake to make.'

Teresa was smiling; Adolph did not look at her.

Gordon now knew he had to be careful, but also perhaps he could have a little fun while he was at it. Or, maybe, he could change Adolph's opinion of Warley Place and the people who looked after it.

As they strolled up the drive towards the turning circle, he explained that he was not a botanist, but a retired engineer, so they might have more idea what some of the flowers were than he did. Nevertheless, he was happy for them to ask if they did have any questions.

He pointed out the Headache Tree, noting that its leaves could cause a headache if crushed and smelled.

'What was the Cardinal's Walk?' asked one visitor, pointing at the remains of a gate and a notice just beside the tree.

'The area there used to be what was called a Pleasaunce,' explained Gordon. 'It was a large lawn, planted with shrubs and flowers. The Cardinal's Walk was simply a path round it, just gravel as far as we can tell, with a brick edge in places as you can see.'

'Why cardinals?' asked Adolph.

'I've no idea,' admitted Gordon. 'The name is taken from a 1904 map. I know the family had quite strong Roman Catholic connections, but I wouldn't have thought they would themselves have named the path for that reason. Have you any thoughts?'

Adolph hadn't, so they continued round the turning circle to look at the cellar and to discuss the old house. Turning back on themselves, they looked at the Walnut Tree, comparing its current appearance with that on an old photograph.

'Just be careful,' he said anxiously, as several of them went right up to the low fence and looked down at the trench on the other side of the ha-ha, a vertical wall on one side of a deep ditch designed to keep animals such as deer or cattle away from the garden itself.

They carried on to stop by the old stable block. He pointed out the Paper Mulberry tree, *Broussonetia papyrifera*, a tree that was not particularly pretty but was once used to make paper and cloth from its bark.

'Where does it come from?' asked Teresa.

'China, Japan, all the countries in that area,' he answered, noting with amusement that Adolph was nodding in agreement when he almost certainly had no idea beforehand. 'Now to the Orchard Garden,' he continued as they turned to file up a narrow path. 'This whole area used to be allocated to growing food plants, hence the name. but Ellen Willmott changed it to a more colourful area full of interesting shrubs and flowers.'

The whole group was attentive and full of questions and comments, just the way Gordon liked it. He wondered if Adolph had decided to keep quiet or if he was waiting for an opportunity to redeem himself.

Gordon pointed to an open-topped galvanised tank, sunk into the ground, with a wooden guard round it.

'That's a dipping tank,' he noted. 'Ellen Willmott apparently used to mark plants needing to be watered, then the gardeners would dip their watering cans in and follow her instructions. There are about twenty altogether, and one day one of our wardens found a couple of dead voles in one of them. When we came in next, we found that he had made little ladders and fitted them in every one of the tanks!'

They moved on.

'She was in some of the RHS committees, wasn't she?' asked one of the group.

'Yes, I believe so. She was certainly on the Narcissus Committee,' said Gordon. 'In fact it caused something of a stir because she joined the RHS in 1894 and was elected to this committee only three years later.'

'She was also on the Lily Committee,' said Adolph.

'So she was,' said Gordon.

'She was elected in 1933, only a year before she died,' he continued in a loud voice, making sure all could hear.

'You have a good memory,' said Gordon. 'Audrey le Lièvre again?'

'Yes, I do know quite a bit about Ellen Willmott.'

'Interesting, though, that I have a copy of the RHS Lily Yearbook for 1932, which lists the committee members for that year,' said Gordon, his forehead creased. 'And Ellen Willmott is among them. That is a year earlier than she was reported to have been elected. I wonder how that came about?'

Gordon wondered what would happen next. Adolph was obviously very interested in the subject and could have been a very useful person to have in a group, perhaps filling in when he himself was uncertain of the answers to some of the questions. However he did seem rather full of himself.

'Audrey le Lièvre's book is excellent,' he continued. 'She obviously did an enormous amount of research, but some of the material she looked at may well have been wrong. And if you have seen Ellen Willmott's writing then you would forgive anyone for misreading a date or a name from her records. Of course, since the book is so good, most of us do quote from it and are usually right.'

Adolph made no comment but, Gordon thought, he looked a little pensive.

They carried on past the old cold frames, then stopped briefly at the remains of a group of hothouses where he pointed out the *Sabia yunnanensis latifolia*, one account noting that Ellen Willmott was the only gardener in Britain to have been able to grow it. Unfortunately it wasn't particularly pretty, the flowers being very small and not very colourful.

They continued to the old nursery beds, a reservoir, and then into the walled garden, which was in full bloom at this time of the year. The various species of daffodils were out of course, but also scilla, few-flowered leek, white and pink cardamines, *Akebia quinata* flowing over the box hedge, cherry blossom, camellias and magnolias in flower – it was just a complete riot of shape, size and colour.

Teresa and the others were full of questions about the trees, and particularly the many different flowers, the names of which he could mostly recall, but some he could not.

They reached the exit to the garden and Teresa gasped as she looked at three daffodils. They had blue edges round the tips of their trumpets.

'They aren't Pheasant's Eye narcissi, are they?' she asked. I've never seen anything like them.

The others were all scratching their heads too.

'No,' said Adolph. 'Pheasant's Eye have red edges and smaller trumpets, don't they?'

He looked at Gordon, who winked at him. Adolph immediately understood, and grinned, no doubt grateful for the tip off.

'Yes, the ones I've seen certainly do. These are unique,' said Gordon. 'I don't think there are any like them anywhere else.'

More gasps.

'However, I think ... I'm sorry, I don't know your name,' said Gordon to Adolph, having narrowly avoided calling him that.

'Harold.'

'I think Harold knows what they are.'

Harold bent down, looked closely and smiled.

'Felt tip pen, rather than paint, I think,' he said. 'Or perhaps a highlighter. On ordinary wild daffodils.'

'Correct.'

The group burst out laughing.

'In some gardens,' explained Gordon, 'visitors have been known to dig up unusual bulbs and take them home. I doctored them last weekend when some enthusiasts came round, but to my delight, as you can see, they were left alone.'

Actually, he noticed, three had disappeared since he coloured them.

They left to examine the remains of the old house, of which little was left apart from foundations, a cellar and the conservatory.

They had a look at what was left of the basement kitchen, wondering at the conditions of working down there, especially with little light other than from acetylene, or, later, towns gas lighting, electricity not being available there in Ellen Willmott's time.

The conservatory, where she spent a lot of her later years, was now just a shell with no doors, no roof and no windows, and a crumbling mosaic floor. They walked through, and turned to walk along the herbaceous border on the outside of the walled garden, then round the corner to a terrace and the daffodil bank – a huge area of daffodils, and later bluebells.

Gordon looked anxiously at his watch, wondering if he was taking too long and boring the group with his chat.

'If anyone has had enough, they can go back to the gate that way,' he said, pointing to the path leading past the Spanish chestnuts. 'But the tour does extend past the daffodil bank and the boating lake, before coming back to this point. It takes twenty minutes – or half an hour if I talk too much!'

'I'm all for the full tour,' said Harold, much to his wife's amazement.

'Me too,' came a chorus from the rest.

So off they went, astonished by the enormous number of daffodils, entranced by the snake's head fritillaries, impressed by the enormous but empty boating lake, and looking a bit weary as they climbed the final hill up to the terrace.

After admiring the view of London from the Spanish chestnuts, finding the superb display of purple toothwort by the gorge, wondering at the enormous stones forming the alpine garden and visiting the hide overlooking South Pond, they made their tired way back to the gate where Donald was looking pointedly at his watch, an amused expression on his face.

'I thought you'd gone,' said Gordon.

'I had. I've come back for my afternoon stint. A bit early, so Daphne can have some lunch, I think she's staying all day.'

Then, to Gordon's amazement Harold came up to him and shook his hand.

'That was very interesting,' he said.

'If you want to come round and see what the public don't normally see,' said Gordon, 'just let me know. We can roam off the paths and do things that you can't do in a larger group. I'd enjoy accompanying you – you are obviously very well read and very interested, so I could learn something new.'

'I'd like that,' said Harold. 'Thanks again.'

As they left Donald appeared.

'Well?' he asked.

'I don't know when it happened,' grinned Gordon. 'There are now only three daffodils. I really wish I could see what happens next year when someone expects to see his daffodils with blue-edged trumpets.'

'It will be even more interesting if he sold them to someone else and they see what they've really got,' laughed Donald. 'Oh dear, here come the bird-watching photographers.'

Actually the volunteers liked photographers visiting because they quite often spotted, photographed and identified things that volunteers had missed. On open weekends, however, parking was at a premium and they did tend to stay for some time.

'We'll be looking for the Seagulls soon,' Gordon said to Donald, once the camera-laden visitors got close.

'Did you know that the correct name for a seagull is actually just 'gull'' commented one of the twitchers, overhearing the remark.

'No, it's definitely 'Seagull'' said Gordon.

The photographer pulled out his bird book.

'*Narcissus* 'Seagull',' explained Gordon. 'And we've got some 'Albatrosses' too.'

The photographer put his book away, sighed and moved on.

'You really must stop teasing visitors like that,' said Donald. 'They might take offence.'

'I suppose so,' said Gordon. 'But I get a bit bored sometimes.'

'How do you tell the difference between Seagull and Albatross daffodils then? They are both white with small yellow trumpets.'

'Well Albatross have a thin red tip to their trumpets. Seagull have a red tip too but only for the first few days after the flowers show, then it disappears.'

'Ah,' said Donald, 'so if I see one with no red tip it's a Seagull more than a few days old?'

'Er…. usually,' grinned Gordon.

'What do you mean by usually?'

'I don't know. The experts who said that didn't elaborate!'

5

A Tentative Approach
July 1934

'I wonder if I could speak with your Mistress? If it is not too early in the day, that is.'

The butler, Robinson, smiled at the conservatively dressed silver haired man who stood before him; medium height; slim build; pleasant but no memorable facial features; it all added up to someone you could pass by without even noticing them. Except that there was something about him. The way he addressed a butler as an equal, not as someone down the social scale who should do what he was told; the way he smiled, a genuine smile that said what words could not; the way, Robinson knew, he was ready to accept a negative answer with understanding and not an argument. All those impressions, those thoughts, took only a second, two at the most, to register.

'It is already late in the day for Miss Willmott,' he answered, but not unkindly. 'However, even if she were here she does not answer to callers without an appointment.'

'I understand,' said Edward. It was over a month since he had escorted her home so she had probably forgotten all about him anyway. He turned to leave.

'May I enquire the nature of your business with Miss Willmott?' asked Robinson. 'I will inform her of your visit and if she wishes I will contact you to make an appointment. Have you a card?'

Edward turned back and passed his card to Robinson, who examined it. His brow creased.

'I doubt whether Miss Willmott would need any plumbing or heating work carried out Mr Saxon,' he said.

'Oh, no, I apologize,' said Edward, taking the card back and retrieving a pencil from his pocket. 'It is a personal matter.' He scribbled his home address on the back of the card and returned it to Robinson. 'I met her a few weeks ago and she invited me to call. I really should have written first. Perhaps you could let me know when would be convenient, if at all?'

'Certainly sir,' said Robinson.

Edward took a step towards the North Lodge.

'Excuse me sir.'

He turned back once more.

'Have you been through here before?'

'Only once,' answered Edward, 'and it was dark at the time.'

Robinson's eyebrows rose.

'I had escorted Miss Willmott back home when concerned about her safety,' explained Edward. 'She offered to show me her garden at some convenient time.'

'Oh, that was you? It was very kind of you. I am sure she will get back to you very soon. Meanwhile may I suggest that you continue down the drive and exit by South Lodge. You will get an excellent view of some of the shrubs and trees as you go.'

It was just a little unfortunate that the garden was at its least colourful in the mid-summer; the spring flowers never failed to evoke cries of admiration and the autumn was rich in more peaceful hues but, although there were many plants to impress those with some knowledge of botany, this time of the year was not one for the casual visitor.

'Thank you kindly,' said Edward, taking Robinson's advice. He had indeed gone that route when he left Miss Willmott at her house but, as he told Robinson, it was dark and he had seen very little.

Bordering the drive was a single row of very mature trees on his left, beyond which was a meadow and still beyond that the main road to Brentwood. His father had told him many years ago that the carriage drive on which he walked had once been the main road into Brentwood, but it had been diverted at the request of the then owner. That would explain the extreme ages of the trees along its edge. He must have had considerable influence with the council, thought Edward.

The overhanging trees made the path a little darker than he would have liked. On his right the ground rose for a bit as he walked down the sloping path and was much more densely populated with trees and shrubs. Some of these shrubs were rhododendrons, he could see that, but they had finished flowering and had lost their power to astonish with their beauty.

Suddenly the shrubs fell back towards a pond and the meadow opened up to his left. It was the pond that drew his attention – or rather the man kneeling tending to some flowers on the border. He must have heard Edward's feet on the path, for he rose to his feet, rubbing his knees, and turned towards the intruder. He was small in stature and had a welcoming, if slightly nervous, smile under a luxuriant moustache that drooped down each side of his mouth. He wiped his hands on his rather faded blue apron as Edward approached.

'I came to visit Miss Willmott,' explained Edward, 'but the butler reminded me that I should have made an appointment. My name is Edward Saxon.'

'Yes, she is very particular about who visits,' said the gardener. 'I am Jacob Maurer.'

Edward couldn't quite place his accent. Possibly German? Or perhaps Swiss. 'You are obviously one of the gardeners?'

'Yes. Well, in effect the only gardener now, apart from one or two assistants, although I was originally employed solely for the Alpine garden.'

'But a garden of this size must need dozens of gardeners.'

'Indeed it does. But for one reason or another it seems Miss Willmott is unable to provide them. But I've said too much. She is in the Orchard Garden at the moment.'

'Jacob!' came a high pitched voice from somewhere among the shrubs.

'Well I thought she was in the Orchard Garden,' muttered Jacob. 'No doubt she's found something I should have done but haven't. I can't be everywhere though.'

'I'm here, by the pond,' he called out.

'Who are you talking to? I heard voices.'

A rather dishevelled figure holding a trowel came through the bushes.

'And who are you?' came the sharp query. Then, more softly, 'Oh, it's you Mr.... Saxon, wasn't it?'

'It is indeed. I must apologize for intruding. I came to ask about seeing your garden and another private matter but I can see you are busy so I will be on my way.'

'No, wait a moment,' she said. Then 'Jacob, you have remembered my visitors at three o'clock have you not?'

'Yes Miss Willmott.'

'You may get back to your work.'

'Yes Miss Willmott.' He wiped the sweat from his

53

brow with his handkerchief and bent down once more with his trowel.

'Now what can I do for you Mr Saxon?'

'There were two things,' said Edward with uncharacteristic nervousness, heightened when he saw her face change. He knew immediately she was suspicious of him, wondering if he was after money, or to gain some other advantage.

'The first was to ask if I could indeed look round your lovely garden at some stage. But I can see how busy you are and it can wait until a more suitable time. I have left my details with your butler.'

She nodded.

'The second thing is a little more difficult to explain. I would like to come and work for you in the garden. I do not wish for payment.'

Her mouth opened a little, but the suspicion was still there.

'Why?' she asked.

'I am a Quaker,' he said. 'But I have had reason to question my beliefs. Normally someone in my position would ask for a Meeting for Clearness at which my concerns would be considered and advice given. However I think I would learn much by working in an environment such as this, away from all external influences. My wife has died and my son has left home to join the Royal Air Force. He has done so with my blessing, if not my full agreement with his reasons. I would like to think about this and many other things, but not sitting in my home alone.'

'The Royal Air Force?'

'My son? Yes. He wishes to fly.'

'And you. Work for no payment? Why?'

'I have a small business which is run by others very efficiently, leaving me with ample means to provide for myself. I neither need nor want payment. In any event my knowledge of gardening is very limited indeed, and non-existent regarding the rare species which I understand you grow here, so payment would not be appropriate although I hope to be of some use. My reward would be in learning about them.'

Ellen Willmott stood there motionless, her eyes focussed somewhere else in time as well as space. Edward waited, comfortable in the silence, until eventually she spoke.

'Come back at three o'clock,' she said. 'I shall be showing a party round my garden and you can join them. Wait at South Lodge and follow Jacob. If after the tour you still want to work here then you may.'

She turned abruptly and walked up the drive towards her house.

'I may see you later then,' he said to Jacob.

'You will if you join the tour,' Jacob replied, turning his head but not rising from his knees. 'When she says she will be taking a tour, she really means I will be taking a tour!'

'But you don't have time to do that.'

'No,' said Jacob, grimacing. 'I've tried telling her that, but it doesn't do any good.'

A strange woman, thought Edward as he made his way to the gate; one who would not allow herself the luxury of doubt, nor that of showing more than a modicum of warmth to others. She must be very insecure, he told himself. He wondered why he had seen only the one gardener when there was an obvious need for many more. The fellow, Jacob, must have been exaggerating when he said he was almost alone, he couldn't possibly manage a garden of this size without a great deal of help. Perhaps he would see them in the afternoon.

Briefly considering a lunch in the Thatchers public house by the gate, he decided instead to walk the short distance home and enjoy a sandwich in comfort and maybe have time for a short nap afterwards.

Was he doing the right thing in working at Warley Place? What good would it do? He had always been a Quaker and it had served him well over the years, leaving him content in the knowledge that he had done all he could to make the world a better place. But what if the war had been lost? Would the world had been a better place then? What if fascism prevailed in Germany and, perhaps as a result of yet another war, spread throughout Europe? Would it be a better world then? Would he not be responsible for the result merely by means of his lack of action? Yes, he had joined the Friends Ambulance Unit as had many others, a dangerous unpaid occupation, but was this just to salve his conscience? He had an uneasy feeling that he should have lauded his son's decision to join the Royal Air Force and hopefully then to prevent another war. He hated the idea of war and all the jingoism that went with it, but then so did a lot of other very brave people who served in one or other of the services.

Since the very beginning, almost three hundred years ago, Quakers had been pacifists. In the early days they would submit to beatings without presenting any defence, so strong were their feelings. But then there were no aeroplanes that could fly high in the air and drop bombs, even on civilians, nor machine guns that could mow soldiers down as a scythe cuts the grass. And who knows what further evils the future would bring.

By the time he got home his head was buzzing, but he was sure of one thing: he needed to clear his mind of all he had been taught. Quakerism was about taking responsibility for one's own actions. Working with nature, tending God's own creations, would provide that clearness. Wouldn't it? But regardless of all the reasoning his instinct told him that it was the right course of action to take, and his instinct had rarely been wrong.

'Come on old friend,' he said as he opened the door and reached for the lead hanging on its nail. 'Just time for a quick walk before we eat.'

Rufus lifted his big head, looked at Edward and seemed to think about it. Then, somewhat reluctantly, he heaved himself off the sofa, shook himself and slowly ambled clear of the softly falling filaments.

'I might be leaving you on your own soon,' said Edward, ruffling the hair on Rufus' head. 'Perhaps you will be able to come too, but I doubt it.'

A casual passer-by might have wondered who was taking who for a walk as they made their way towards Headley Common. There Edward would let him off the lead, but he never went far and couldn't be bothered to run if walking would get him where he wanted to go. They were just good company for each other. Rufus was someone to talk to; companionship, especially now Howard had gone, but even before that. Edward was just someone to provide food and warmth, that's what some people said, but he knew that Rufus enjoyed his company for more than that.

'She's a strange woman, that one,' he said.

Rufus turned his head towards him, then with a bored look turned away again.

'Very confident on the outside, but there's a lot of insecurity inside. She hides it with impatience, intolerance even. Not an easy person to work for. Impossible to live with, I imagine.'

They reached Great Warley village green and the Thatchers inn, right next to the gates to Warley Place and South Lodge, Jacob Maurer's home.

'Jacob's so different,' he continued. 'Genuinely confident, so much so that he doesn't feel he has to prove anything. He's happy with his lot in life. I like him.'

Rufus investigated the base of the tree with the pub sign hanging from a bracket nailed to its trunk, then lapped some water from the horse trough.

'OK, home we go,' sighed Edward. 'My goodness it's hot!'

He let his thoughts wander on the journey home. He was happy with the idea of working at Warley Place. He tried to think about what he might be asked to do; he tried very hard. But thoughts of Howard up there in the sky kept flooding back. He had seen those flimsy machines falling from the heavens, often flames licking over the pilot, his arms flailing to beat them away. The lucky ones were motionless, slumped against the controls. At least they had parachutes now though.

Arriving back at his cottage, Edward paused to look at the little front garden. His wife had always kept it neat and colourful and he did his best to continue that way. He was gradually beginning to recognize which were weeds and which were cultivated plants as they poked their heads through the soil, but still found it difficult at times.

Edward was strict with his dog, feeding him mornings and evenings only. Well, except when cheese was in the offing. As he sliced the cheddar for his sandwich, a certain amount did end up gulped down by Rufus, who then wandered back to the sofa for his afternoon sleep.

'Sorry Rufus,' said Edward when he swallowed the last piece of bread and drained his glass of water. 'I'd love to join you, but I'm going back to Warley Place and if I shut my eyes I'll go to sleep and be late. Who knows, maybe you can come some time, but not today. Anyway, it's cooler inside.'

He checked the bowl of water.

'Bye Rufus,' he opened the door.

His dog's eyes were already shut.

6

The Research Group Investigates
May 2013

'Remember when you first came and were nervous of the Research Group?' Ken reminded his wife as they parked their car in the little car park just inside the reserve.

'Yes, and I still am a little,' admitted Elsie. 'They know so much more than I do about plants.'

'You underestimate yourself,' Ken said. 'They just know different things than you do. And your drawings are beautiful. Ellen Willmott was good, but even she would have been envious.'

'If I hadn't plucked up the courage to come in, we'd never have met,' she said. 'That one decision changed my life.'

'It changed mine, too,' he said, squeezing her hand.

'Never mind, you'll get over it,' she laughed.

Ken and Elsie had set up a small specialist plant nursery nearby as an adjunct to his parents' larger one, with Elsie illustrating many of the plants that they sold. The monthly walk round Warley Place with the Research Group was one of the few outings they managed to get together, as normally one or other of them needed to be working.

Other cars started to arrive, until nine members of the group had gathered round Deirdre, the leader of the group.

'Right,' she said. 'Someone suggested that we try to find some of the features that are shown on the map but are now hidden, starting in the Pleasaunce area. What equipment have we got?'

'I've got a trowel and a fork,' said Anne, who was the scourge of the Japanese knotweed, now rarely daring to show itself in the reserve, and interested in all aspects of the garden.

'I've got an extract of the map showing that area, and a tape,' said Peter, who had a particular interest in the architecture and history of the reserve. 'I've also got some old photographs.'

'I've got a prodder,' said Gordon.

'A what?' asked Elsie.

Gordon produced a thin steel rod about half a metre long with a handle at one end.

'It's for use on people who don't move fast enough,' he explained.

'Don't listen to him,' said Ken. 'It's for prodding the ground to see if there is a path or something solid beneath a layer of earth.'

'That too,' agreed Gordon.

All the others had implements of some sort or another, so they started their walk up the drive.

As was normally the case with this group, progress was at best spasmodic, being disrupted by the frequent examination of interesting plants. They eventually reached the turning circle

'Remember that body we found in the concrete?' Elsie said to Gordon, as they glanced at the walnut tree on the meadow, just the other side of the ha-ha.

'Maybe we'll find another one today,' said Gordon hopefully. 'It made a change from clearing up leaves.'

'I prefer collecting leaves,' said Elsie.

They turned to go through the remains of the iron gateway that formed the entrance to the Cardinal's Walk, and started to make their way back the way they had come, but parallel to the carriage drive.

They were immediately confronted with an apparently impenetrable barrier of shrubs.

'I think we might be starting at the most difficult part,' suggested Peter. 'According to the map the path wriggles its way through shrubs here, and then goes straight across by the retaining wall. If we by-pass it and start at the straight bit we could perhaps trace it back to the gate.'

'That seems sensible,' said Deirdre, so they moved across into the main area, past the remains of a monkey puzzle tree. Their way back to the path was still blocked, this time by a spread of rhododendrons.

As they worked their way round them, Deirdre stopped at a stump, but one that had shoots growing out of it.

'I thought that was dead,' she commented.

'It's a Laurel, isn't it?' said Gwen, a long standing member of the group. 'It's amazing how it's survived.'

'Very amusing,' said Gordon.

'Amusing?' queried a suspicious Deirdre.

'It's a Laurel – and hardy,' explained Gordon.

'Don't minute that,' said Deirdre to Sally, who was taking notes and well used to not minuting Gordon's remarks.

A short distance further on they came to the dwarf brick retaining wall, no more than half a metre high, dropping down to a further much smaller area. The wall was in a reasonable state in some places but in others crumbling away.

'That's nature at work,' commented Peter.

'What was it?' asked Ken. 'Just a lawn?'

'No, it's shown as a bowling green on the map, but I believe it was also a tennis court,' said Robert. 'I've also got some photographs showing Frederick Willmott and others apparently using it to play croquet on.'

'That's right,' said Peter. 'Not much chance of using it for that now.'

What was once pristine grass was now covered in trees, rabbit holes, and mounds possibly once mole hills.

Deirdre unrolled her map, and Peter pulled a photograph out of his bag.

'Look,' he said. 'There used to be a large urn right in the centre, half way between the path and the wall.'

The walked the few metres towards where the ornament once was.

'There's its base,' Peter said, scraping the grass away to expose a slab beneath, shaped like a millstone.

'There are several things to look for,' said Deirdre. 'The path, the wall (which we can see), the urn (the base of which we can now see), and two wooden gazebos, one at each end of the wall.'

'There are also some steps shown down to the bowling green at the western end,' said Anne. 'I found them some time ago but they aren't in a very good state. I think we're going to have to restore them.'

'I'll see if I can find the path with my prodder,' offered Gordon.

'I'll look for the remains of the gazebos,' said Peter.

The group split up into groups of two or three to look for the various items shown on the map, and Robert, the group's unofficial photographer, removed the lens cap from his camera and started scribbling in his note book.

Robert and Peter walked along the wall to towards the drive and were confronted with a small but dense patch of shrubs. They set to work with some loppers and a saw.

'How are you getting on with your French friends,' asked Peter. 'And how are they getting on with their book?'

Robert had some time previously met three women from France who were independently searching for archive material to help with a book one of them was writing. Ellen Willmott had bought a chateau in Tresserve, a village near Aix-les-Bains in Savoie, in 1890 and owned and visited it until about 1920, when she was forced to sell – something that almost broke her heart, as she loved the house, its gardens and the area. However the building was now the Mairie, or council offices, of Tresserve and a local group were trying to restore part of the garden to what it once was. One of them, Geneviève, was writing a book about it. Much information had passed each way, from them to Robert and vice versa and a very friendly relationship had developed.

'Actually the book is complete now. It's called *La Mairie de Tresserve* and should be out soon. I'm looking forward to seeing it. Very little of it has been taken from *Miss Willmott of Warley Place*, so it should be very interesting.'

'Let me know when it's available, I'd like a copy,' said Peter, pulling sawn-off branches out of the way and peering into the remains of the rhododendron.

According to the map the path ran parallel to the wall, on the other side of the urn. Gordon and Ken were busy with the prodder, poking the ground where they thought it would be, with ambiguous results.

Anne and Elsie had taken trowels to the west end of the wall and were scraping away, unearthing the steps which appeared to be constructed of cobblestones, many of which had come loose from their original positions.

'Are you OK doing that?' Deirdre asked Elsie, her forehead creased.

'Yes, I'm fine, thanks. Baby's not due for a few months yet. Well actually September, so four months to go.'

'Well if you are sure, but don't overdo it.'

Sally and Gwen had taken loppers and were trying to find the gazebo at the opposite end from where Robert and Peter were working, but having similar results.

For twenty minutes or so all that could be heard was the sound of tools scraping, sawing or digging, together with the occasional 'Ouch!' as a barbed shrub objected to being disturbed. Eventually first one group, then the rest, congregated at the urn.

'Well there is a path,' said Gordon, 'but it seems to be just a gravel finish. It's not paved, so although we exposed a few feet it doesn't seem worth exposing the rest. It would just be more work for volunteers to maintain it.'

They all looked at the exposed section and, a little disappointed, had to agree.

'Perhaps one day,' said Deirdre, 'but a long way down the list of priorities I would have thought.'

'There is no sign of the gazebo foundations at the drive end,' said Peter. 'It's hard to be certain because of the shrubs, but I suspect it was just a wooden structure on bare earth, which is what the photographs suggest, in which case it would have long since rotted away and was probably doing so in the latter days of Ellen Willmott's reign.'

'Same with us at the other end,' reported Anne. 'We think it was probably where the Summer House now is, and she built it when the old one disintegrated.'

The remains of what was called a Summer House comprised just three brick walls, one oval window opening and no roof. Perhaps one day the volunteers would find a use for it.

'The steps down to the bowling green are still there though, basically in very good condition, but as Anne said, they do need to be reconstructed,' said Elsie. 'They aren't safe at the moment.'

They all walked to that end of the wall and sure enough, the cobble-like steps were in good condition, although loose and a little uneven because of subsidence. Anne demonstrated how wobbly some of the stones were, and suggested that until they were stabilized the steps should not be used.

'Well, that was a useful exercise,' Deirdre summarised. 'We've found where the urn was, we've found the steps, we know the path was just a gravel one, and we can confirm that there is no trace of either of the original gazebos.'

'The bricks on the retaining wall will need a lot of re-pointing, or more likely dismantling and rebuilding' said Gwen. It would be a great shame if we let it collapse.'

'I'll ask David if we can spend some time on it,' Peter said.

'Interesting that it's called a Rose Bank on some of the pictures,' said Robert. 'Some of them show just a grassy bank, some of them have some flowers that don't look like roses although it's hard to be sure, but none of them show the wall like it is now. If it was a bank, I wonder why the wall was built?'

'So many things we still don't know,' commented Deirdre.

'We may get some answers from Geneviève's book,' said Peter. 'Robert tells me it's coming out very soon.'

'Oh that is great news,' said Deirdre. 'Do we know when?'

'Well actually it's next month,' said Robert. 'There is a book launch at Tresserve. They've asked me to go, but I only just scraped through O Level French over fifty years ago and didn't keep it up. I'd feel terrible not knowing the language.'

'Do you mean you've never been to France?'

'Well, no,' admitted Robert, 'I haven't.'

'You'd be mad not to go. They would look after you. And isn't one of them English anyway?'

'Yes, Jo is English and living there for the moment, but I couldn't expect her to translate everything for me.'

'But most of them speak some English. It won't be a problem. You'll regret it if you don't go,' insisted Deirdre.

'I know,' said Robert. 'My wife told me the same thing.'

'Right. That's settled then. Tell them you are going! Right, what's next on the agenda?'

Sally looked at the agenda.

'The rockery,' she said. 'Anne would like us to identify a plant she's found.'

'We haven't looked at the wiggly bit of the path,' noted Peter, looking at his map. 'Perhaps we should try to walk along it to get to the rockery?'

This proved easier said than done, the shrubs having spread and weeds grown to the extent that it was soon impossible to trace the original path, even with energetic use of Gordon's prodder.

'I think if Peter and I come on our own we could mark out the edges with bricks as far as possible, then we can all decide how far we go in cutting back if we want to reveal it all,' Anne suggested.

'Good idea,' Deirdre agreed. 'It's a waste of time all of us poking around here. We can finish it next month.'

The distance from the Pleasaunce to the rockery was approximately 100 metres but distractions were plentiful so it took the best part of half an hour to continue that distance. Moving carefully between the sharp rocks bordering the path round the rockery Anne crouched down and pointed to a little yellow flower with five petals poking out between two rocks.

'I do believe that's a *Saxifraga cymbalaria*, or celandine saxifrage,' said Deirdre thumbing through her book. 'Yes, here it is. Quite rare in England in Ellen Willmott's time so just the sort of flower she would have planted. It's not common now either, but because it spreads fairly easily in the right conditions some people call it a weed. And one of the right conditions is a rockery like this.'

'But there aren't any others here,' said Robert, so where could it have spread from?'

'Well, birds drop all sorts of things,' said Deirdre, 'but it would be a coincidence if they dropped something just here. Some seeds might have lain dormant since her time I suppose. We'll never know. But it's well worth looking after.'

Sally scribbled away in her notebook and looked at her watch.

'It's getting on a bit and I've got to go soon.'

'I think we've seen all we planned to see, so we might as well call it a day,' suggested Deirdre.

Once back on the path they turned and made their way towards the car park.

'Getting back down to basics,' said Gordon as they strolled along, 'we've got a lot of periwinkle here, but some have pointed petals and some have petals with flat ends. What's the difference?'

'I think we've got three sorts of periwinkle,' said Anne. 'Some of them have much smaller leaves than the others.'

'That's right,' said Deirdre. 'We've got Vinca major, the ones with the flat-ended petals; we've got Vinca major oxyloba, which are the ones with the pointed petals. That's what oxyloba means. And we've got Vinca minor, with the smaller leaves. It's not quite that simple though, and it might take some time to find examples of all three and we can look closely at them.'

'What are we looking for in identifying them?' asked Gordon.

'Oh, the size of the calyx lobe, whether the leaf margin is ciliate, length of calyx hairs, that sort of thing,' she explained.

'I thought it might be that,' said Gordon, rolling his eyes. 'Another time then?'

'Another time,' agreed Deirdre. 'I suppose there's nothing in your archives about vinca, is there Robert?'

'No, Anne already asked me that question. Nothing dating back to Ellen Willmott, anyway.'

'We've not found any vinca labels, either,' said Anne. 'I suppose that's not surprising, it's almost a weed.'

'We'll have to get something done about that Hornbeam,' said Deirdre, looking at the very old specimen on the side of the drive. 'If the top grows too much it could topple on a wet and windy day. It's several hundred years old and worth looking after.'

It was a job for a professional, so Sally noted it down for the minutes.

'It's sad,' said Peter as they opened the gate, 'to think that this car park used to be covered in Jacob Maurer's greenhouses.'

'I bet he used to hide here from Ellen Willmott sometimes,' grinned Gordon. 'Or at least did some propagating as a rest from digging up weeds.'

Replacing their boots with shoes, they sat on the back of their cars, each with his or her private thoughts, before setting off for home.

7

A Garden Tour
7 July 1934

'I must go now Maggie,' said Jacob to his wife, gulping down the last of his mug of tea. 'Can't keep the old girl waiting or I'll be in trouble.'

Jacob had married Rosina from his native Switzerland. She who bore all his children, but died of tuberculosis in 1918 shortly after the birth of Iris, their ninth. He had been married to Maggie for nine years now. She was the daughter of the couple who ran the bothy in which he lived with other unmarried staff when he first came to Warley Place. She loved his children and they loved her.

'You have to do everything now Jacob, it's not fair.'

'There's no-one else left, is there,' he said ruefully. 'My old bones won't take much more of this and I'm looking forward to retiring but there's not much hope of that yet. We need the money too, I've got an awful feeling about the pension she promised.'

'Don't say that dear, I'm sure you'll get something, and surely we won't get thrown out of here?'

'What are you going to get up to while I am out?' he asked, changing the subject.

'A nice pie for tonight, I think,' she replied. 'With the children grown up it's nice to be able to just do what I want in the afternoons.' She smiled to herself, then her eyes opened wider. 'Not that I minded when they were young, I loved looking after them.'

'I know you did, my dear,' Jacob reassured her. 'They know you loved them and they all love you.'

'And I love them still,' she said, 'and always will.'

Few women would have taken on another woman's nine children and loved and cared for them in the way she had done. He was very lucky indeed, he reflected, and so were they. Poor Rosina had so little time with them. His eyes moved to the window.

'Oh, I see that man's arrived, the one I told you about. I think he's come to join the Field Club people I've got to show round.' He gave a little groan and rubbed his knees as he rose from the chair.

'Good gracious,' said Maggie, 'As if you haven't got enough to worry about.'

Everyone always used the back door of the cottage, and as Jacob came round the corner he saw Edward at the gate looking round uncertainly. He noticed Edward's face lighten when their eyes met.

'Hello again,' said Edward extending his hand as Jacob reached him. which Jacob took with a firm grasp. There was a short pause and just as Jacob realised Edward had forgotten his name he added 'Jacob'. Jacob smiled at the look of relief on Edward's face at remembering and immediately liked him for his sensitivity. 'I'm sorry, I don't remember your last name,' Edward continued.

'Don't worry,' said Jacob. 'It's Maurer. And you are Edward but I too forget your last name.'

'Saxon.'

It's strange, thought Jacob, but there are some people to whom one takes an instant liking. He knew straight away he would get on with Edward, were he to see him again.

'Have you been here long?' asked Edward

'For forty years,' answered Jacob. 'I came here in' – he screwed up his eyes and thought – '1894. I used to work with Henri Correvon until Miss Willmott asked me to come here to look after her Alpine garden.'

And perhaps I should have said no, he immediately wondered. On the other hand he was working on what he considered was now the greatest alpine garden in England and probably further; its fame was not only due to the expensive plants Miss Willmott provided, it was also his expert care that made it so special. And she really was a talented gardener, he conceded, even if she seemed to have little interest in her staff's welfare. She certainly had little patience with Preece, her head gardener for twenty years but who was asked to leave in 1911 and who died in the flu epidemic in 1918. On the other hand she did her best for Thomas, the water engineer, all those years ago. Until comparatively recently she'd have been on holiday somewhere or other for a good part of the year, so things were much better then, but lately she spent most of her time at home, interfering.

'Henri Correvon?' asked Edward.

'Oh, sorry, Mr Saxon. He was a Swiss botanist from Geneva. She bought plants from his Jardin Alpin d'Acclimatation and one day saw me working there. I was nineteen years old at the time and this seemed like a great opportunity and an adventure. You know how simple things are at that age. She promised me a small pension and somewhere to live when I retired, and the chance of working in what was likely to become the most acclaimed garden in the country. I couldn't resist.'

Ah, he must be Swiss himself then, thought Edward. That explained the accent.

'Please, would you mind calling me Edward? Everybody does.'

'Things are rather formal here and I don't think Miss Willmott would like me to do that. You are a visitor and I must call you Mr Saxon. I would be pleased if you would call me Jacob though and I will call you Edward if we meet outside these gardens.'

'But what if – '

'I see the other visitors have arrived,' broke in Jacob. 'They are from the Essex Field Club. Miss Willmott is a member. She will be in the alpine garden already and won't like being kept waiting.'

'Hello Mr Maurer,' said one suitably attired lady who seemed to be leading the group as they made their way through the main gate. 'This is Miss Prince. There are thirty-eight of us today, I hope that is not too many. My goodness it's hot.'

'Good afternoon,' said Jacob. 'Miss Willmott asked this gentleman, Mr Edward Saxon, to join you for the tour. I hope that is in order.'

'You are most welcome,' she said, turning to Edward. 'Are you a botanist?'

'Er, no,' said Edward. 'A business man who has often wondered what was behind these walls but sadly with a limited knowledge of horticulture.'

'Your first visit then. I'm sure you will be very impressed.'

'What are all those greenhouses for, behind the little cottage?' asked one elderly gentleman as they gathered round Jacob.

'They are plant nurseries, mostly for the Alpine Garden,' said Jacob. 'There are other greenhouses too, some heated, but further on past the house. We may get time to see them later on, but maybe not.'

More likely not, he thought, bearing in mind the state they were in.

He turned and led the party up the drive past the pond, briefly explaining its previous use as a watering place for horses on what was once the main road, before turning left up the slope to the alpine garden. He turned to make sure everyone was following and smiled as he saw that Edward had trailed behind the group and was looking at a startling display of flowers with a very puzzled expression; he obviously could not recognize a single one of them.

Jacob melted into the background when they reached Miss Willmott who was standing on the stone bridge that crossed the gorge. There were enormous rocks everywhere; on either side of the bridge; round a small pond to his right; lining the gorge; all about them. Jacob often wondered how on earth they could have been hauled up the slope, let alone placed in such positions; most of the work had been completed before he arrived at Warley Place. The flowers that grew between them, right down to the small stream that trickled along the bottom, were astonishing in their beauty and never failed to move him, even though he saw them every day.

The buzz of conversation stopped suddenly as Miss Willmott started to speak. Jacob heard the words, but it was her usual welcoming speech that went in one ear and out of the other, as did the fawning response from the visitors.

'Today you will see my alpine garden and also the walled garden, and of course the path between the two. Possibly the Pleasaunce, but it is a little hot to walk round the rest of the estate this afternoon, but perhaps on another day.'

Very nicely done, admitted Jacob. The rest of the estate was in such a state she wouldn't have wanted anyone to see it. The greenhouses were positively dangerous and the brambles and nettles were everywhere. Planting Japanese knotweed and Himalayan balsam had been a daft idea; it had spread well beyond the point at which it could possibly be controlled, as had the bamboo in some areas, and the giant hogweed was a menace.

'So I will leave you with Jacob and meet with you to say goodbye when you have finished. Jacob?'

He slowly walked to the front. Oh how he hated this duty. He just wanted to get on with tending his plants. His accent didn't help, and when he was nervous he had a slight stammer. She always stood there for a minute or so while he started. Why didn't she just go?

'I will show you round here first,' he said. 'If you have any questions please just ask them. I like to do it as a friendly chat rather than a lecture. Does anyone have anything to say before we start?'

There was silence. He hated silences. It was all right on his own, when he was tending the plants and thinking his own thoughts, but with a group of people all staring at him it was horrible. He prepared to move when a voice spoke up.

'Who designed this beautiful garden? And who constructed it? These rocks are huge.'

Jacob looked in surprise and relief. It was Edward who was speaking. He was the last one Jacob expected to hear from.

'James Backhouse of York designed and built it to Miss Willmott's specification and under her supervision,' said Jacob. 'Getting all these rocks into their chosen positions was an enormous task and I am sorry I was not here to see it so am unable to say exactly how it was done.'

Oh well, let's get it over with, he thought to himself.

'There are rather too many of us to get down amongst the plants in the gorge,' he said, 'and it would not be safe for the less nimble among you so we will confine ourselves to certain individual plants that we can see from the path while we move to the pond below.'

He was relieved to see Ellen Willmott move quietly away, probably to the conservatory where she spent most of her time these days.

'I can hardly tell you anything new about flowers,' he went on, so I'll leave you to enjoy them.'

'What a collection of campanulas,' noted one member of the group.

And she was right.

'The *Raineri* is an interesting one,' noted Jacob, pointing to a small delicate looking plant with funnel shaped lavender blue flowers. He could see Edward looking puzzled, so continued, 'It's so different from most other campanulas that some people would wonder over its identification.'

He watched as the club members wandered about looking at what took their fancy, and then saw Edward. He had his hand on one of the rocks near the path, his face slightly puzzled and a little sad. Seeing Jacob he looked at the flowers.

'What is that one?' he asked, indicating a small yellow-flowered plant in amongst the rocks.

'That's a *Primula sikkimensis*,' answered Jacob.

How strange, he thought, that this stranger should pick on the very flower that Alex had also queried all those years ago, and who had also made his presence felt on Ellen Willmott.

'From Sikkim' I assume?

'Yes, but also Nepal and Yunnan. It's got a good scent,

and quite long lived, so a good plant to have in such a rockery.'

'I asked Miss Willmott if I could work here,' Edward said. 'She said if I still wanted to after this tour then I could. I'd like to. I hope that would be all right with you?'

'Yes of course,' replied Jacob. 'The help and the company would be very welcome.'

'What is this plant then Mr Maurer?' came a voice from further down the path. As he hurried to see which plant they were pointing at he glanced back, to see Edward once more running his hands over the rock. Jacob felt the hairs rising on the back of his neck.

The group's questions came thick and fast after that and they were soon walking along the path past a forest of foxgloves, leaving the alpine garden behind and looking down at London in the distance through the seven Spanish chestnut trees.

'The *Narcissus triandrus* were lovely earlier,' Jacob said. 'And still pretty in fruit.' They stopped briefly to look at the tall *Umbellularia californica*, or Headache Tree, at the corner of the walled garden. Miss Willmott always liked to show this to her visitors. If the leaves were crushed and smelt they would often bring on a severe headache, but if they were used in an infusion they would cure or ease one. There were two of these trees, the one they were looking at and the other by the turning circle.

Walking slowly along the herbaceous border, they turned into the walled garden itself, admiring the *Ginkgo biloba* tree and the *Magnolia obovata* – its flowers gone but its huge leaves still evident – then the myriad of flowers of all sorts of sizes and colours.

The Wig tree, *Cotinus coddygria*, was also noted with its yellowy feathery flowers looking like puffs of smoke – hence its other name, Smoke tree.

Jacob's mind was on other things and he was glad when Miss Willmott finally joined them in time to introduce them to her Woad plant (*Isatis tinctoria*). Three feet high it was in full golden flower. Blue dye, she explained, had been obtained from the leaves for centuries.

One of the visitors turned towards the northern exit from the walled garden.

'I think we have time to take the Cardinal's Walk,' said Ellen Willmott quickly, moving towards the southern exit. 'We could have gone round the boating lake, and I'd be happy to do so at a later date, but spring is by far the best time of the year for that particular part of the garden.'

Edward smiled to himself. Having had a quick look through at the greenhouses just to the north, he knew full well why they were going back south.

Jacob led the way to the Headache Tree by the turning circle, beneath which was the iron-gated entrance to the Pleasaunce, a grassed area with a gravel path around the perimeter.

As they filed through, one of them remarked on the Monkey Puzzle tree, an old specimen, tall and with triangular pointed leaves.

'*Araucaria araucana*,' said Ellen Willmott to the unspoken question. 'Not my favourite tree, but rare enough, from Chile.'

The path wound its way through low shrubs, the names of which either Ellen Willmott or Jacob noted as they passed.

'That's an odd looking rhododendron,' said one.

'That's because it's not one, it's a *Trochodendron aralioides*,' said Ellen Willmott. 'It does look a bit like a rhododendron, but the flowers are completely different, bright yellowy-green with no petals, just long stamens. Some people say it's the loneliest plant in the kingdom – a single species, in a single genus, in a single family. It's also more of a tree than a shrub. Quite rare.'

It was interesting, thought Edward, that although he normally abhorred a show of pride in possessions (for wasn't pride a sin?) he found it unable to be other than pleased for her at that moment. In fact, he decided, it wasn't pride she was showing – it was pleasure at being able to grow something that would otherwise be in danger of extinction.

They continued their short diversion until they returned to the conservatory, at which Ellen Willmott politely made it clear that the tour was at an end.

There followed the usual thank you speeches and cold drinks, after which they left for Brentwood Station to return to their homes.

'I trust it went well?' asked Ellen Willmott, as Edward admired the Garden House at the corner by the entrance to the walled garden.

'It seemed to,' confirmed Jacob.

'What do you think of Mr Saxon?'

'He seems very interested. I believe he may be working here shortly? He would be a good asset if he did. I could do with the help.'

'Then if he wishes to, he shall.'

There was a moment's silence, then Jacob, somewhat nervously, spoke.

'He was paying a lot of attention to Alex's stone,' he said.

She stopped, her eyes focussing on something in the distant past.

'And he asked about the *Primula sikkimensis*.'

'So?'

'That was the first plant I showed Alex when he came,' Jacob explained. 'And he keeps stroking the rock. The one that – '

'Coincidence,' she said, cutting him off and turning to look at Edward.

'Mr Saxon?' she called.

He walked over and smiled.

'What do you think? Do you want to join us?'

'I should be most pleased to do so, if you will have me.'

'Then you shall. When can you start?'

'Monday, the day after tomorrow?'

'Monday it is then. Report to Jacob, but I will show you round before you start working.'

Edward turned and made his way to the main gate. He knew this was going to be an interesting experience, and wasn't that what he was after? Deep in thought he walked past the Thatchers public house, briefly noticing two men huddled over a table. One had a red and black kerchief round his neck. He hurried on.

'You really don't like him, do you Bertie?' said one, noticing his companion looking at the receding figure.

'Nah. I almost 'ad the old girl. Just had to snatch 'er bag and be gone. Then 'e came along with 'is bloody dog.

'I fear your *modus operandi* needs improvement. Besides, there was probably little of value in it.'

'Modus what? I wish you'd speak English Nige'

'And I wish you'd call me Nigel, not Nige. I like to practice my Latin. My old dad told me that if I learned a few Latin phrases I could impress people, and in my line of work that's what I need to do.'

His line of work was in fact swindling people out of their money, but his reputation was getting to be too well known and he would soon have to move further afield.

'Well, what's it mean then?'

Nigel sighed.

'Method of working,' he said. 'You should have just done it, not kept thinking about it. *Fortes fortuna adiuvat.* Fortune favours the brave.'

'Yeh, well that's the trouble, I ain't very brave. I don't wanna go inside again, it weren't nice.'

'Look, we know the old girl has lots of very expensive stuff in that house of hers; we know she lives there alone; we know the place is falling apart. Getting in would be easy. We just need to know where to look.'

'Yeh, I know all that.'

'I have a plan.'

'You all right Nige... sorry, Nigel?'

'What?'

Bertie sniggered. 'You didn't say that in Latin.'

'Any more of that and I'm out of here and you will miss out on more money than you can imagine.'

'OK. What is it?'

Nigel looked about, and lowered his voice.

'The whole place is a mess, isn't it? She can't get gardeners. Can't afford them, so I hear.'

'True.'

'Well I offer my services, free of charge, on approval like, and worm my way into her confidence.'

'You'd be good at that,' admitted Bertie. 'But you don't know nothing about gardening.'

'I did a spell once in a very highly regarded garden and a highly regarded owner,' Nigel said. 'It was hard work though. Too hard. They were taking advantage of me, so I left.'

'You mean they caught on what you were up to,' said Bertie.

Nigel ignored him.

'They won't want me doing complicated stuff. I'll soon have her wrapped round my little finger. Everyone likes being told what they want to hear, and if I smile at them and do that, they'll believe anything. She'll soon be feeling sorry for me when I nearly pass out with the after-effects from my war wound, and let me in the house. I can find out where the jewellery is. Maybe I can leave a window unlocked. Then one night we come back and do it. The next day she'll be crying on my shoulder.'

'She'll never fall for it.'

'It's what I do. Con people. It's easier than you think. My dad taught me well, God bless him.'

'Your dad died in prison after someone sussed what 'e was up to.'

'Yes, but that in itself was a good lesson. The main thing, so he told me, was to tell people what they want to hear.'

'Yeh, then when they find out you ain't told them the truth they thump you!'

'No, you can always blame someone else, and folk don't like to admit being fooled, even to themselves.'

'So what yer doing next?'

'I start helping out.'

'How?'

'I just walk in and ask.'

'Forty fortunes an' that' said Bertie.

'What?!'

'Fortune favours the brave. You said it earlier.'

Nigel cringed. He'd have to keep Bertie well out of the way until that night.

'*Ad Meliora,*' he said as he rose from his seat. 'Just keep out of trouble. I'll let you know when you need to be involved.'

'When you want some mug to take the risks,' muttered Bertie under his breath.

'Towards Better Things,' explained Nigel over his shoulder as he left.

8

Une Visite à Tresserve
June 2013

Robert watched Stansted disappear behind the wing as his Airbus A319 lifted off the runway and cleared the M11 motorway by – well, actually not by very much, he thought. He didn't mind flying; in fact he enjoyed trying to make out the landmarks as they passed over them, but hated all the palaver at the airport prior to boarding. Presumably it helped to keep the cost of the flights down, but everything seemed to be geared to extracting as much money from the public as possible before they boarded – if they had any left that is, after paying parking charges. However, now the stressful part of the journey was over he was able to relax.

After a few minutes watching the clouds, he reached for his French phrasebook. Fortunately the seat next to him was empty, so he didn't feel too self-conscious. They'd said to him that it didn't matter that he didn't speak French, but he knew they really appreciated someone trying. He'd worked in the Netherlands once, many years ago, and tried learning Dutch. Because he worked there his pronunciation became quite good, but he never managed to converse with a Dutchman in that language. He remembered one phrase even now, '*Ik Nederlands verstaan als u langzaam spreke, maar als u vlug spreke dan verstaan ik u niet*'. 'I understand Dutch if you speak slowly, but if you speak quickly then I don't understand you.' He had tried it just the once and was treated with a warm friendly smile and a reply in Dutch, spoken slowly but still incomprehensible. The Dutchman then spoke perfectly good English and said most of them preferred to speak English so that they could practice it. So '*Je comprends le français si vous parlez lentement*' wasn't on the list of phrases he intended using! His English friend Jo, who would be meeting him at Lyon, had given him a useful sentence to use though. '*Excusez-moi je ne parle pas très bien le français.*' '*Merci*', '*s'il vous plaît*' for 'thank you' and 'please' would also be useful and he remembered those from his schooldays.

He closed his phrasebook and opened it at a random page.

'*Where is the nearest campsite?*' '*Où se trouve le camping le plus proche?*'

Oh no. He hoped he wouldn't need that. He opened it at another page.

'*Which platform does the train leave from?*' '*Le train part de quelle voie?*'

Why was he bothering? Geneviève and Claude were very friendly indeed and Geneviève spoke good English. But he was staying with Claude, and Henri, her husband, neither of whom did. On the other hand Jo and her husband Irwin would be there a lot of the time and they were British. It would be fine. Wouldn't it? Of course it would be fine – but he was ashamed at how poor his French was at school and that he had not attempted to improve it in over fifty years since.

He wondered how Ellen Willmott had travelled to Tresserve. The boat across the channel of course, but from there? The train probably, but she had written about her chauffeur Frederic, and how he never picked her up on time, and how fast he drove on the roads, so perhaps he drove her from the ferry. More likely he just did the local sight-seeing trips. He'd not seen any reports of her flying, but there was a service from London to Paris just after the war flying converted First World War bombers, so he supposed she could have done. Not with all the stuff she usually took with her though, he decided. Anyway, the early flights only went to Paris and she'd still have to get from there to Aix-les-Bains, some way further south.

Did she speak French? Almost certainly, considering the time she spent there, but she seemed to spend a lot of her time with English compatriots, most of whom seemed to have 'Lady' or 'Sir' in front of their names.

She had loved Tresserve enough to consider selling Warley Place as early as 1910 when her finances were at a low ebb, and moving to France, but her ties with Warley were too great and she couldn't bring herself to do so. She struggled on for ten more years until finally she sold her chateaux in Ventimiglia and in Tresserve, and stayed in Essex. Actually her finances continued to be dire from then on for the next 14 years, going from one crisis to the next, until she died.

The two engines changed their note and, as the aeroplane started its descent, it broke through the layer of clouds, and Robert gasped. He was sitting on the left side and saw what he assumed were the Alps appearing. He'd seen the Scottish mountains from the air, and those in Ireland, but never anything like these snow-capped peaks. His eyes were glued to the window until the aircraft's wheels thumped on to the Lyon runway and the reverse thrust pushed him forwards in his seat.

He sat there for a few minutes while a number of

impatient passengers pushed their way to the exit, then he followed them after a self-conscious 'merci' to the flight attendant at the door, immediately wondering if she was English. Lyon was not a large airport and, in an unaccustomed short time, he had collected his bag from the carousel and found his way to the exit. He soon spotted Jo and Irwin waving to him from behind the gate, and after another short walk he was sinking into the back seat of the car.

Irwin and Jo said they would take a diversion when driving back to Tresserve, going along the edge of the Lac du Bourget, the deepest and largest lake in France. Robert had seen Loch Lomond in Scotland, which too was blessed with mountainous surroundings and was somewhat larger than this stretch of water, but even Queen Victoria had been very taken with what reminded her very much of her beloved Scotland. She paid several extended visits to Aix during the late eighteenth century and her birthday, 24th May, was still celebrated there. Lough Neagh in Northern Ireland was many times larger, greater in area even than Loch Lomond, but did not take his breath away as this one did. There was simply too much to take in; the enormous lake, the huge range of mountains on the far side, the buildings, the gardens, everything was amazing and his head was spinning by the time they reached his friends' flat for a meal.

After a brief visit to their apartment and a quick meal, they took him to drop his bag off at Henri and Claude's house. A large but unpretentious enough building from the outside, he was amazed when he entered to find how far it stretched. After a warm welcome, Henri took him along a corridor and showed him to his room, far bigger than his own in England. Henri explained in simple

French how the heating worked and so on, giving him ample practice at using *'oui'* and *'merci'*. The view from the window was spectacular, with the mountains in the distance dominating everything.

They then left for the Mairie, where a meeting of the Patrimoine, the local history society, was to take place. It was dark by then and little could be seen of the outside of the building, so they quickly went in and he took his place next to Irwin and Jo near the back of the small hall – the small hall, Robert suddenly realised, being one of the rooms of Ellen Willmott's old house!

Robert knew that a Mairie was a sort of town hall, and even the small towns or often villages had, and still have, one. The building is usually a notable one, often the most impressive one in the area, and in this case Ellen Willmott's old house fitted the bill. The maire (mayor) was very proud of its history and so were the inhabitants of Tresserve. The house itself dated back to the mid-17th century, bought by Ellen Willmott in 1890. She loved the house and the garden, developing both to her own taste and visiting often. She could not actually afford to keep it going and was not able to return after 1913, renting it out instead and neglecting its upkeep. Eventually her sister Rose and her husband Rob Berkeley persuaded Lord Berkeley, a distant relative, to buy it in 1920. Lord Berkeley never went there and, in a sad parallel with Warley Place, the house and garden were neglected and reclaimed by nature.

There was no mention of Tresserve in Lord Berkeley's will when he died in 1942, probably he had forgotten he owned it, and French law resulted in its ownership being in some dispute. Eventually a family moved in and carried out improvements, but in 1957 a compulsory purchase order was raised and work carried out to convert it to a working building, and in 1961 it was inaugurated as the Mairie for Tresserve.

Although now used as offices and meeting rooms, as much of Ellen Willmott's furnishings and character as possible were retained, and this was obvious to Robert as soon as he walked in.

Apart from his name, Robert understood very little of what was going on after being introduced to everyone, but was happy to immerse himself in the 'French experience', including a superb informal meal afterwards, during which he had to demonstrate that the wax coating on the Wensleydale cheese that he had brought was not edible!

Eventually it was time to leave, and as he walked back to his house he reflected on how friendly they all were, and tried to remember their names so that he could thank them properly. Alain, he remembered, because he spoke to him in English and told him what was going on during the meal, but few others apart from Geneviève and Claude who he already knew.

When he got back he was shown to his bedroom again by an attentive Henri, who reminded him where the bathroom was. He was asleep as soon as his head hit the pillow.

The following morning he took another long look at the beautiful view from his bedroom window. Instead of the houses he normally saw from his own window in Brentwood there were mountains, including the distinctive mountain, La Dent du Chat, on the other side of the lake and the snow-capped Alps, he assumed, in the distance. A relaxing breakfast, including coffee made as only the French can make it, was made even more enjoyable by him and his host Claude, whose husband had left early, trying to communicate when neither could understand the other's language very well. Instead of being embarrassing, as he had feared, it was very enjoyable indeed, with much laughter and thumbing through a dictionary.

Jo and Irwin then picked him up and they first stopped at the Mairie to see it in daylight. He got out of the car and just stood there, spellbound. It wasn't the beautiful view of the mountains, or the lake itself, or even the impressive Mairie. The grounds, sloping down towards, but not reaching, the water's edge, were well cared for but not packed with the flowers that would have been there in Ellen Willmott's day, so it wasn't that either. He just had the strange feeling that she was there next to him, coming back to see her old property and liking what she saw. He understood now why she had considered leaving Warley Place when times were difficult, moving back to Tresserve to spend the rest of her life there. It was all so tranquil, so beautiful. The grounds were far smaller than those at Warley, but the setting would have more than made up for that. There was now no direct route to the lake itself but it seemed that there was a path once.

Eventually he roused himself and was taken round Aix-les-Bains, and what a surprise he got. Apparently Queen Victoria's youngest daughter Beatrice suffered from rheumatism even in her twenties and in 1883 her doctors sent her to Aix-les-Bains to 'take the cure', as the locals called it, in the baths. Her condition was very much alleviated for the first time and on her second visit she accompanied Queen Victoria herself for three weeks. The queen made two further three-week visits, one in 1887 and another in 1889, travelling over in her yacht and then her own railway carriages to the local station.

There was some talk of Beatrice buying property in Tresserve at this time and it may or may not be a coincidence that Ellen Willmott bought her chateau in Tresserve in 1890.

The local people were delighted that the British queen came, because it encouraged so many other visitors to do the same. After the first visit the name of the street along which she travelled from the station was changed from Rue des Soupirs to Avenue Victoria.

Robert saw signs of her visits everywhere; the name of the hotel Villa Victoria; the plaque of Beatrice in the courtyard of the Hôtel de l'Europe; bust of the queen in Place du Revard and many other reminders. There was a regular guided walk round the town 'In the Footsteps of Queen Victoria'.

After doing a mini version of the tour and then visiting the market, they got back in the car and drove down to the lake where they had a good meal with a fantastic view and he practiced his *s'il vous plaît*'s and *merci*'s.

Then finally back to Claude and Henri's house where he got washed and changed for the presentation of Geneviève's book.

It was still light when he got to the Mairie and he had time to wander round the garden to examine some of Ellen Willmott's original planting, and to photograph the outside of the chateau. Once again he had the feeling that she was there, willing him to see it as it was in its heyday, especially as he walked along the avenue of plane trees planted by her early in her time there and included in her photographs.

It was with some reluctance that he went back inside to speak to people, still embarrassed at his almost non-existent French, and to wonder at the way the building had been refurbished to make the most of its previous owner's lavish spending on fixtures and fittings.

The next couple of days flashed past. A hair-raising drive up the La Dent du Chat to get a view of the lake below, only to find that they had climbed into the clouds; a visit to the Savoy Hotel in Le Bourget du Lac to stand where Ellen Willmott photographed friends having tea on the balcony overlooking the lake; a visit to the La Serraz chapel to take a picture from the same spot that she stood to take her own photographs; a guided tour with Geneviève round Tresserve itself and another round Aix with Jo to see where Queen Victoria stayed and played. Then suddenly he was standing once more at the Lyon airport waiting for his flight home, wishing firstly that he could stay another week and secondly that his French was better so that he could have made even more of his time there. But one thing was certain – he felt that he knew Ellen Willmott more than he ever could have done from just looking through dusty archives and faded photographs.

9

Edward has a visitor
8 July 1934

Edward put down his book and looked at Rufus, who had lifted his head from the sofa and was looking, with a faintly irritated expression, at the door.

'I think we know who that is on a Sunday afternoon, don't we Rufus?' Edward commented, pushing himself up from his chair and walking along the short passage.

'Hello William,' he said before the door was fully open. 'On your own?' he continued, looking up the path.

'On my own Edward,' his visitor responded with an amused smile on his lips. 'This is just a friendly visit.'

'Friendly with a small or capital 'F'?

Quakers called each other by their name or just 'Friend' – and a 'Friendly' visit was usually carried out by two elders or overseers of the Society of Friends to help to iron out any problems the subject may have. This concern went back to the beginnings of Quakerism, when so many Friends were incarcerated or worse because of their beliefs.

'A small 'f' I promise,' said William. 'You have not been to Meeting for two Sundays running, and I hear Howard has joined the Royal Air Force. I wondered if you wished to clear your mind and if I could help. However if you have no such need I shall bid you farewell and until we next meet.'

'I am not sure that you can help, but I should be glad of your company, and thank you for your concern.'

Edward ushered him into the small front room and into the chair he had just vacated. Rufus politely wriggled along a bit to let Edward sit next to him on the sofa, then placed his only slightly drooling mouth on his owner's lap.

'Woolman.' said William looking at Edward's book. 'He makes me feel so inadequate.'

'Me too,' smiled Edward.

They settled into a silence, the short period of quiet that Quakers often found themselves immersed in before they tackled a problem of any significance, or maybe just a discussion. It was broken not by any predetermined time or a signal from one or the other, but by an unspoken agreement. Probably, in this case, also by a snore from Rufus.

'Howard joining the Royal Air Force has indeed made me think,' said Edward. 'But I cannot find it in me to condemn him for it. To be ready to fight to prevent a greater evil, in the hope that it may prevent that evil from taking place, surely that cannot be so wrong? He has searched his conscience and it is clear to him.'

'It goes against all our teachings from our very beginnings,' replied William. 'Conscience provides us with a sense of duty originating in human society, whereas the Light within us is illuminated by absolute God-given standards of right and truth. And that Light tells us that violence and the killing of fellow human beings is wrong.'

'They are grand words,' said Edward slowly. 'Violence and killing is of course wrong. But those words were written in the days when individuals killed each other one by one, face to face. Now machines fly high in the sky and drop merciless bombs killing dozens, maybe hundreds, of unsuspecting citizens below. Clouds of gas, big guns firing from miles away, kill without the perpetrators ever seeing the results. Surely it is not wrong to try to prevent that?'

'I disagree with you,' said William. 'But I have to admit that your son is not the only Quaker to have followed this path. The Friends Ambulance Unit was an honourable compromise in the last war and I was hoping it would be so in the next, although some say it just releases others to do the fighting instead of the caring.'

'The FAU was manned by very brave men and they did great things. I served with them, but was never called upon to do what many of them did. But they could not prevent the war, only relieve the suffering. What Howard wants to do is to prevent it ever starting.'

'Yes, of course you served with them and I understand why. But what if Howard fails?'

'Then he will do his duty to try to finish it as soon as possible.'

They sat in silence, each thinking of what the other had said and whether either of them was right or wrong.

'Will you take some tea?' asked Edward eventually.

'Will your dog allow you to make some?' asked William, smiling.

Edward eased Rufus's head from his lap and went to the kitchen where he put the kettle on and washed his hands.

'I am going to work for Ellen Willmott of Warley Place,' he called out.

'Ellen Willmott? Good gracious. But you already have a thriving business.'

'I know. I want to do something different.'

'Well you are joining an illustrious group of people, going right back to John Fothergill and Upton Park.'

John Fothergill was an 18th century Quaker, a philanthropist and physician, but also a plant collector who built up an interesting and sizeable collection in a garden which later became West Ham Park.

'No,' chuckled Edward, 'I could never be a botanist. I just want to help with the menial work. Weeding, collecting leaves, turning the compost, that sort of thing.'

'How much would she pay you for that?'

'I'm not doing it for payment. I just want to do something different; enjoy a different environment that will give me the time and space to think.'

'You can do that here, or at Meeting for Worship.'

'No. Here I am tied to the past; to all the books I have read, the people I respect, the memories I have. I want to set them aside for a while. It is easy for one to ignore facts that disagree with our ingrained beliefs and only accept those that reinforce our position. I hope this will enable me to do just that.'

He thought for a moment.

'And anyway, she needs me.'

'What? Ellen Willmott needs you to turn her compost?'

'No. I don't know what she wants,' Edward said, putting William's tea on a small table by his chair. 'I don't think she knows, either. But she is very disturbed and appears to have no-one to confide in. Perhaps she won't confide in me.'

'I can hardly imagine you getting on with Ellen Willmott. You could hardly be more different. I gather she let a fortune pass through her hands on a garden and property in Italy and France, when it could have been put to helping the poor.'

'She employed a lot of poor people in this area,' said Edward,. 'She could have spent it all on holidaying and just living a life of luxury. Also,' he continued, 'her gardener is having a very difficult time, that is not hard to see. He has problems with his joints and faces an impossible task with the garden. I may be able to help with the garden in some small way, and he too is troubled about the future. Not that he has said as much, but it seems so.'

'She may have employed a significant number of local people before the war,' said William, 'but she was also rather a spendthrift, so I understand.' He paused, uncomfortable at criticising. 'But yes, I believe she did also do her best for refugees and disabled soldiers when they came home. I still cannot understand why she might need help though.'

'I understand what you say,' said Edward. 'I can't explain it, even to myself, I just feel it to be so.'

'Well,' said William thoughtfully, 'you have had those mystical feelings before and been right. It's hard to imagine in this case, but God be with you.'

'Thank you dear Friend.'

Edward hesitated.

'But I am afraid I am no longer even sure that there is a God.'

William froze, shocked for a moment.

'Oh dear. I had no idea things had gone that far. Why do you doubt?'

'I don't know. I do not believe that there is not a God. It is just that I am no longer sure that there is one. I think it is the unfairness of life. Not for me, I have been fortunate, apart from the death of my dear Margaret.'

'So you no longer believe in a life after death?'

'It is possible, I suppose, that there is no God but there is still some form of life after death; or there is a God but no life after death; or no God and no life after death. But, dear Friend, I have not said I believe there is no God or no life after death. I simply no longer know.'

'Do you not feel frightened at the prospect? All right, the possible prospect?'

Edward thought for a moment.

'No,' he said. 'Just a little disappointed and a little sad. It will not affect my outlook on life here on earth one bit. Anyway, being frightened of something shouldn't be a reason for not believing it.'

They sat for a few minutes in silence, considering what each other had said, before William rose to take his leave.

'I hope you will still feel able to attend our Meetings for Worship,' said William. 'Even if your thoughts are not clear at the moment, they may become so.'

'Thank you dear friend for your visit,' said Edward as he saw William to the door. 'Do not concern yourself about me. If nothing else, I expect I shall be fitter than ever I was before, and be newly acquainted with the world of gardening. And yes, I would certainly look forward to attending Meeting.'

Edward settled down again to his book. Until his death in 1772 John Woolman had fought for the meaningful abolition of the slave trade and had written:

> *"Many Groans arise from dying Men, which we hear not.*
> *"Many Cries are uttered by Widows and Fatherless Children, which reach not our Ears.*
> *"Many Cheeks are wet with Tears and Faces sad with unutterable Grief, which we see not."*

Woolman had been referring to slaves and their families, but the sentiment applied also to the poor and otherwise disadvantaged everywhere.

He put the book down. So what on earth was he, a Quaker who believed in simple living, doing trying to help someone who had, as William had said, got through a fortune almost entirely spent on her own gratification, and a gardener blessed with a place to live, a wife and nine healthy children? What about those whose faces were sad with unutterable grief?

10

Une Invasion Française
July 2013

Robert waited at the Stansted Airport international arrivals with some trepidation. Eight of the people he had met in Tresserve were visiting Warley Place, and he was there to guide the minibus they were to hire to their respective lodgings. Four of them were to stay with Deirdre, the leader of the Research Group, and three with Daphne. Jo, their British translator, was to stay with Robert.

He hated airports. Flying, he enjoyed, but the airport experience he found to be stressful and boring at the same time. From the time you parked your car to the time you left, no opportunity was missed to part you from your money. It was deliberately boring, to force the poor customers to visit the shops. Another delay? Then why not buy another coffee, or a book, or some presents for your husband or wife, or your friends, or even for yourself?

To his relief the flight was on time and they poured through the gate towards him.

'*Hello Robert, ça va?*' said Claude.

'*Ça va bien, merci,*' he replied, having looked up the likely greeting in his book the previous day and hoping it wouldn't be taken as an invitation to continue in French. Improving ones vocabulary and learning a few verbs and phrases was all very well, but it had been impossible for him to practice common conversation. Someone had said once that the ordinary person's biggest fear was looking a fool in public, and trying to speak French was very much in that category for Robert.

Jacques was looking around, presumably for the car hire desk, so Robert pointed it out to him. *'Le bureau est là,'* he said pointing it out.

'Yes, I see it thanks,' said Jacques in perfect English, much to Robert's relief.

It was soon apparent that they all spoke English to varying degrees except Claude who struggled. Robert warmed to her, empathising with her being in a place where everyone spoke rather fast in a language she could not follow. Not long ago he had been in the same predicament and she had been very understanding. He had at one time dabbled with Esperanto, the proposed universal language, but there seemed to be very little scope for its use so he'd given up fairly quickly. What language should a well-meaning Englishman learn? French? German? Russian?

After a few minutes small talk, during which Robert kept a close eye on certain members of the party who were eyeing the shops too intently for his comfort, Jacques came back from the car hire desk and waved them towards the exit and the car park.

A minibus had been pre-booked, and they made their way towards it and Robert's car, which was parked close by. The minibus had a satnav and Robert gave Deirdre's post code to Jacques, although the plan was that he would follow Robert's car. They were soon driving down the M11 motorway and then to Ongar and on to Deirdre's house. Geneviève, Claude, Jacques and Françoise stayed there with the minibus and Alain, Anne, Jo and Ghislaine got in Robert's car for the journey to Daphne's house. After passing through Ongar and driving towards Brentwood, Alain laughed out loud and pointed to the notice by the road. 'Secret Nuclear Bunker', it said. 'Not so secret now,' laughed Alain. 'Have you been inside?'

'I have,' said Robert, watching out for deer, who seemed to have no road sense and were as likely as not to run out into the road from the trees, 'It's quite scary to think that the government thought it necessary to build such things.'

After driving through Brentwood and dropping the three off with Daphne, it was getting late before Robert finally reached home with Jo, who was ready for a quiet evening and looking forward to not having to translate anything for anybody.

It was with some trepidation on the next morning that Robert awaited the arrival of Geneviève, Claude, Jacques and Françoise. He was to take them to the town centre where they would meet up with Daphne's contingent to see Ellen Willmott's grave by the side of the Brentwood Roman Catholic cathedral, before going on to the St. Mary the Virgin church in Great Warley before lunch and then the Warley Place tour. Sure enough, when they parked and Robert's few met up with Daphne's, their eyes wandered to the shops. A quick look and a promise that they could spend more time later if they wished, and they were ushered to Ellen Willmott's grave. It was marked with a simple plaque, and had a few plants growing on it, but was otherwise unremarkable.

Geneviève looked at the plaque.

'Frederick was her father, yes?'

'Yes,' confirmed Robert.

'So where is her mother?'

'She is buried at a different place, not far from here. We don't know why.'

'Perhaps because she was dead?' said Alain.

'No, I meant....'

'It is OK Robert, I jest. We understand,' laughed Alain.

'There is nothing in the archives?' asked Geneviève.

Geneviève had been one of the group who had examined some of the archives at Spetchley Park.

'No, nothing,' said Robert. 'We are trying to find out. No-one seems to know for certain, but it seems that at one time there was a plan to move Mr Willmott to join Mrs Willmott. It did not happen.'

There was not a great deal else to look at, so with some shepherding help from Daphne they were soon off to park in the small Warley Place car park at Great Warley. Robert knew that the few days planned were just not going to be enough, but he also knew he was going to enjoy them.

They walked to the St Mary the Virgin church and were all enamoured with the Grade I listed building. Its remarkable and beautiful Arts and Crafts and Art Nouveau interior made them gasp with surprise and delight as they passed through the door. Mother of Pearl was widely used in its decoration, but also materials such as marble, various metals and walnut furniture. Daphne explained that although not old, built in 1902, it was one of only three Art Nouveau churches in the country and probably the best preserved of those. The original church had been located further south, but it fell into disrepair when the village gradually moved to higher ground. After a few years using a temporary wooden church in the Rector's grounds, this new church was built with money and land donated by the Heseltine family.

Wishing that they could have spent more time there, they walked back to Warley Place to enjoy, after a very pleasant lunch at the Thatchers, the main reason for their visit.

Walking just a few paces from the pub, Robert pointed out Jacob Maurer's old cottage, South Lodge. They were all amazed that Jacob, his wife and nine children could be accommodated in something so small – although Robert wondered if some of the older children might have left home before the youngest arrived. Iris, Jacob's youngest daughter, had once commented to Robert that she could only ever remember being happy there, even though they only had oil lamps and a single battery-powered radio. Perhaps Jacob's home-made wine had something to do with it! More likely the amount of time they spent playing in the open air, although they were never allowed to wander in the main garden.

Making their way to the small car park, the two meadows came into view. Fortunately Daphne, Deirdre and Peter all had better French than Robert and most of the group spoke English, so he contented himself with comments made usually after surreptitious looks at his notebook.

'*Au printemps il y a beaucoup de jonquilles,*' he said self-consciously. Being June, the daffodils had long since disappeared.

They straggled up the drive, wondering at the old trees that lined it when it was the main road to Brentwood, and stopping to look at South Pond, imagining the rocks and flowers that used to crowd around it.

Robert had compiled an illustrated summary of what they would be seeing, complete with a very brief description of each item, in French. However his idea of how French ought to be written differed somewhat from the way French people thought it ought to be written, so he anticipated some interesting discussions with Jo, the translator.

Some time was spent by the Headache Tree and the ruins of the house, many of the questions being translated by Jo but many others phrased in excellent English. Warley Place volunteers would have loved to have Ellen Willmott's house preserved in the same way as the Mairie was in Tresserve!

The old Orchard Garden, a few layers of brickwork delineating the cold frames, ruins of hot houses and what was left of the old coach house fascinated them as there was nothing like this at Tresserve. The walled garden was particularly impressive, dominated by the huge Ginkgo biloba tree, and the visitors said they could imagine being Ellen Willmott, walking round keeping an eye on things.

The only difficulty Robert found was keeping some of them from wandering off on their own. Not for the first time Robert wondered about the merits of training a sheep dog to accompany him on such visits. This was particularly relevant when they came to the gorge and the huge rocks forming the old Alpine Garden. It would be very easy to put a foot in a rabbit hole and break an ankle and it was with some relief that they all emerged safe and sound.

Several hours later, with comments being made about how much more extensive it was than they had envisaged, they collapsed into the various vehicles to transfer to Daphne's house to eat and to discuss the next day's visit to Marks Hall and Beth Chatto's garden.

Robert joined his French friends in the people carrier for the journey to Marks Hall, which was much bigger than Warley Place and complete with a walled garden, river, lake, arboretum, and many other plantings. It also had an excellent catering facility, where the group had a very acceptable lunch.

Not far away was Beth Chatto's famous garden, built on a site half the size of Warley Place but packed with plantings on all sorts of soils, including a dry garden. With an energy that astonished Robert, on the way back to Deirdre's house they stopped at a village where the women investigated the local shops, but the men sat and had a quiet drink.

Eventually they arrived back at Deirdre's house and had an excellent meal, looked at Warley Place photographs, and played croquet.

Early the following day, much too soon, it was time to go home and Robert was driving back to Stansted guiding the minibus to its destination. The invasion was over.

11

Edward starts at Warley Place
9 July 1934

Not entirely sure of what to wear, Edward had bought himself a new pair of working boots, some tough trousers, a shirt and a hat to protect himself from the sun on this still very hot day. He assumed that tools would be provided so left his own meagre equipment in his shed.

He had forgotten to ask what time Jacob started work, so decided to be there a little before eight o'clock and about fifteen minutes before that time he picked up his bag containing water, cheese sandwiches and an apple, checked once more that Rufus had food and water in his bowls, and made his way to the front door. He would have to come back at lunch time to let his dog out for a short while, but since he was working unpaid she could hardly object.

Not for the first time he wondered if he was doing the right thing, possibly for the right reasons, or the wrong thing for the right reasons – or even the right thing for the wrong reasons. Oh dear, why did his brain so often lately go round in circles like that? Why couldn't he just trust his instinct? Too late now anyway, he couldn't back down after giving his word. If only Margaret were still here he could have talked it over with her.

He said goodbye to Rufus and left for his day's work.

Jacob was bent down working in the alpine garden when Edward arrived, although what he was doing was a mystery. The gardener looked up, smiled and rose to his feet, holding his back.

'Ah, you've come. Excellent. I think Miss Willmott would like to see you before you start work.'

'I see you have started already. I omitted to ask what time I should be here.'

'The normal time is six o'clock, and we work until six in the evening. However Miss Willmott will confirm that when she sees you.'

Edward realised that Jacob did not know that he was not going to be paid for working there, and there did not seem to be any need to enlighten him. It might just embarrass Miss Willmott, although it would be hard to imagine anything embarrassing that lady.

'Does Miss Willmott start at six too?' asked Edward.

'Often, unless she is unwell or on her travels. And she does her paperwork in the evening, unless she is reading or writing her letters.'

'But I prefer to be in the garden,' came a high pitched voice from the other side of the bridge over the alpine stream.

My goodness, thought Edward, was she spying on Jacob or just happen to be working in the area?

'I gather I am rather late,' said Edward. 'I apologise.'

'Where is your dog?' asked Ellen Willmott. 'Rufus, wasn't it?'

'I have left him at home. I assumed that you would not want dogs in your garden.'

'Nonsense. He is a well behaved and friendly creature and will be wanting to get out exercising himself, not cooped up in your house.'

Edward thought of Rufus curled up on the sofa, enjoying the peace and quiet, but said nothing.

'We have had many dogs here, although not at the moment,' she continued, a little wistfully. 'You must fetch him. Do so and then come up to the walled garden and I shall show you round before you start.'

'That is most kind of you,' Edward said.

'Not kind; you will work better and for longer if your dog is with you.'

She smiled and walked away.

Jacob looked at her departure and when she was a safe distance away he turned to Edward, his eyes wide open.

'She's not done that for a very long while.'

'What?'

'Smiled.'

'Oh, I thought you meant her joke about working harder and longer.'

'I'm not sure that was a joke.'

Edward shook his head, puzzled. He realised that his time here was certainly going to be a new experience. He put down his bag and turned back to the gate.

* * *

'Come on Rufus,' he said, letting himself into his cottage and dangling the lead.

Rufus looked up, thought about it, and eventually clambered off the sofa and let his master fix the collar round his neck. Margaret had commented one day that it made Rufus look like a slave when he was wearing it, so ever since then Edward had taken it off when they got back from their walks.

'You've got to behave yourself Rufus,' Edward said as they made their way up the slope. 'No chasing rabbits or squirrels.'

It wasn't that he stood any chance of catching anything, it was just that he didn't mind what he ran through while he was trying. Edward cringed as he thought of what Ellen Willmott would say if his dog carved a swathe through her herbaceous border.

'And no piddling on her lovely trees. Not in front of her, anyway.'

He knew Rufus couldn't understand him and wouldn't have taken any notice even if he could, but he had always chatted to him like that and always would.

To his surprise, even though he had half expected it, instead of waiting for him in the walled garden she was with Jacob when he returned.

'You may let Rufus off the lead,' she said.

'I am a little concerned that he might damage some of your plants by wandering off, investigating some smell or other,' said Edward.

'There's nothing that hasn't been done by the ravages of time. And nothing that you or Jacob could not repair.'

Edward released the lead.

'Come Rufus,' commanded Ellen Willmott.

To Edward's amazement Rufus dutifully went to her and lolloped alongside when she strode off along the path. He hesitated for a moment, almost waiting for a 'Come Edward' command, then hurried after them.

She pointed out the fascinating Persian Ironwood tree – or *Parrotia persica* as she called it – and a young Spindle tree, *Euonymus*, before coming to a halt before seven huge Spanish chestnut trees. These were the trees he had seen when walking with the Essex Field Club a few days before.

'John Evelyn planted these,' she explained, looking at him to see if he knew who John Evelyn was.

'The diarist? My goodness, they must be old.'

'Oh yes, they are. He owned this estate at one time you know, and visited it although he never lived here permanently.'

Edward said nothing. John Evelyn lived over two hundred years ago, and even to his unpractised eye they did not look that old. His Quaker principles would not allow him to lie, but was acquiescing in something he believed was not true the same as lying? He decided it would be hurtful and fruitless to even try to query what he had been told.

'What a lovely view,' he commented. 'Apart from the smoke over London, that is.'

It was indeed a lovely scene. First across Warley Place's west meadow and its border of trees, then fields and farmland beyond until, as he had pointed out, the smoke obscured much of London's buildings.

'We lived there once,' said Ellen Willmott, a faraway look in her eye. My sister Ada died there. Poor sanitation. It is one of the reasons why we moved here.'

'I'm sorry to hear that. Was she your only sister?'

'No. My sister Rose lived here for a while. She too died, a few years ago. Of cancer.'

Her voice choked a little and Edward could see how close they had been.

'I am very sorry to hear that too,' he said. 'My own wife died of influenza. When someone that close to you dies, your life changes. She is still as near and dear to me as I expect Rose is to you.'

She nodded and turned to continue.

'This is the wall of the walled garden beyond,' she said as they walked along the herbaceous border towards the house. 'It is where I expect you will spend much of your time.'

Just before reaching the house they came across a gate, alongside which was a beautiful brick summerhouse. They walked through to see what must once have been a magnificent enclosed garden, the three main beds delineated by small box hedging. Ellen Willmott pointed out the *Ginkgo biloba* tree, a *Magnolia obovata* with huge leaves, several other magnolias, and several trees the names of which he promptly forgot. Edward, non-gardener that he was, also noted the box needing pruning and the weeds growing in abundance between the flowers.

Instead of following the perimeter path they walked through to the gate at the far side. She fell silent and he sensed a tenseness in her, and when they emerged he could see why.

There were two huge glasshouses on his left, both dilapidated, and a further one at the far end in the same state. On his right was a complex of working buildings, including a large coach house with a spire with a clock face but no hands and a louvre on an adjacent side. It was surmounted by a weathervane fashioned in the style of a galloping horse, tail flying in the wind. A large reservoir dominated the yard itself.

It was the buildings that shocked him though. They were in a poor state indeed, with paint peeling off, doors hanging crookedly and roofs barely weatherproof.

'That's a lovely coach house,' he commented, trying to find something complimentary to say.

'Oh yes,' she said, her face brightening as she remembered. 'At one time we had a Landau, a Brougham, a Victoria, several waggonettes, a pony chaise and a pony cart.'

'That's a lot of coaches. What did you need them all for?'

He closed his eyes. He had not meant to be so forward. However she took no offence; indeed, she accepted it as a compliment.

'We had many illustrious visitors and they needed to be picked up from the station. They preferred a coach rather than a motor vehicle. I had one of those for a while but it was not reliable so I got rid of it.'

She put her hand down and ruffled Rufus' head.

'We had fourteen dogs at the time, as I recall,' she said wistfully.

'Right, on we go. We'll just see the greenhouses and then you can get to work.'

They walked along a winding path alongside the north meadow and past another reservoir, before reaching a number of greenhouses grouped together, sunk partly into the ground. They too were in poor condition and she was not inclined to get closer than the path, limiting herself to just informing him that they were there. He did stop for a moment though and noticed a large shrub growing at the far end of the greenhouses. The state of the structures made it difficult to see whether it was growing inside or outside of their protection. His guide saw him looking.

'*Sabia latifolia,*' she said. Then, with a mixture of wistfulness and pride, 'I believe it is the only one growing in this country. Wilson brought it from China.'

'Wilson? Was he one of your friends?'

'He was a plant collector I sponsored...' she paused, a little uncomfortable, '...I helped to finance his expeditions to China. He died a few years ago but yes, I count him as one of my friends.'

'He must have had some remarkable tales to tell.' Edward did not add that the shrub may well have been rare but perhaps no-one else wanted to grow it because it did not seem, to his unpractised eye, to have any aesthetic qualities.

'I think that is enough for today,' said Ellen Willmott, turning to return the way they had come. 'Perhaps Jacob can show you the rest of the estate at another time.'

Walking back to the house Edward could not help noticing that there were at least two boiler houses beneath the ground, which he could see from the chimneys that rose from them and from the heating pipes within the glasshouses themselves. He wondered how long it had been since the boilers had been fired. Some considerable time, he guessed.

'Jacob will tell you what to do,' she said sharply as she turned to go into the conservatory at the corner of the house. Edward could see that she had perhaps shown more of her feelings than she would have liked.

Rufus stood there, apparently uncertain as to who to follow.

Ellen Willmott sensed something and turned round. She appeared to soften.

'Come on Rufus,' she said. 'You can come with me if you wish.'

Edward did not know whether to be pleased or disappointed as his dog followed her into the house, no doubt to look for a comfortable sofa.

As he made his way back towards the alpine garden he wondered again what he had let himself in for. To keep the garden in the state it deserved would have taken perhaps twenty gardeners; to get it back to that condition from the state it was in now would have taken twice as many. He had seen a couple of men working in the distance, but apart from Jacob that was all. It was a hopeless task.

Jacob grimaced and rubbed his knees as he straightened.

'You are to tell me what to do,' Edward said apologetically.

'From what you've said, you don't have much experience,' said Jacob.

'Well, no. But if you want me to weed and you are worried that I might dig up the wrong thing, just give me a sample and I'll do it. I can recognize ragwort and nettles, and I saw some of both those plants on the meadow as I came in.'

'Do you mind?' asked Jacob. 'It's long and thankless task, and one I've been dreading.'

'Don't worry, it will do me good. If I see anything I think is a weed, I'll bring you a sample and you can identify it for me. Thistles are very common. Ragwort are those tall plants with sort of spiky leaves and yellow flowers on. Have you a wheelbarrow I can use?'

'Certainly, use this one. It'll give me an excuse to go back to my house for another one, and maybe a sip of tea while I'm there. You might need this fork to loosen them, then try to pull them up, roots and all. If they break off, don't worry. Stamp the earth down afterwards, it helps a bit to stop more seeding there.'

'Well, you've started,' Edward thought to himself as he wheeled the barrow across the drive to the east meadow. 'Now we'll see if you are as fit as you thought you were.'

Reaching a particularly tall specimen of ragwort, he bent down and pulled; it didn't budge. Reaching for the fork, he dug it in and loosened the soil, then gave another yank. The plant came out so suddenly he found himself flat on his back looking at the sky, holding his prize over his prone body. As he manoeuvred himself to his feet, he heard laughter, and Ellen Willmott appeared from behind

115

what he later found out was a Hornbeam tree. She was followed by Rufus, who Edward was pretty sure was laughing too.

'I'm sorry,' she said, smiling, 'but I haven't had a good laugh like that for a long time. I think I am going to enjoy your presence here.'

'That's all right,' he laughed.

'I haven't had a good walk round the whole estate for some time, so I thought I'd take Rufus,' she said. 'Unless he wants to stay with you.'

'No, that would be good,' he said. 'It means I won't have to take him out when I get home. I have a feeling I might just want to sit and read before retiring early!'

'You may well.'

She walked back to the carriage drive with Rufus happily loping along by her side.

He moved to the next specimen and not bothering to try to pull it first, he inserted the fork and wiggled it before slowly but firmly easing it from the ground.

After about an hour his wheelbarrow was piled high and he made his way back to Jacob.

'There's lots more to do,' he said. 'Where do I put these? Oh yes, and I left one there because it had lots of little red and black striped caterpillars on it.'

'Oh yes, cinnabar moth caterpillars. They don't do any harm; about the only thing they eat is ragwort – but they don't seem to keep it much in check. The moths don't do much harm either, but they also don't do much good. They don't taste nice so don't get eaten. Best just to pull the plant up and let them finish their meal on the compost heap.' He waved to a hidden spot. 'Just behind there, you can't miss it.'

Edward started to move off.

'How are you feeling?' asked Jacob.

'Oh, fine,' said Edward. 'Nothing to it. No aches or pains. Could do it all day, easily.'

He smiled at the puzzled and slightly disappointed look on Jacob's face, and burst out laughing.

'I'm joking, my knees hurt, my back hurts, my arms hurt, everything hurts. But I'm enjoying it.'

Jacob grinned and kneeled down to continue whatever he was doing – Edward didn't ask, he knew Jacob was glad to be able to use his expertise while the mundane weeding was being dealt with.

'Do we stop for lunch?' he asked.

'Oh, yes, I forgot that,' Jacob said.

'I've bought some sandwiches.'

'Well come and eat them at my table,' said Jacob. 'You haven't met Maggie yet, have you?'

'No, I haven't, and would be delighted, but I don't want to intrude on what must be a welcome half an hour's break.'

'Maggie wouldn't forgive me,' said Jacob. 'She would love to see you. I'll just finish what I'm doing and I'll come and fetch you.'

His late start and his brief tour with Ellen Willmott meant that only one more wheelbarrow-load and a lot of day-dreaming later he was suddenly startled to find Jacob next to him.

'Lunch?'

They left their things where they were and it took minutes to cover the short distance to South Lodge, where Edward was made welcome by Jacob's friendly and motherly wife who insisted that he shared their tomato soup and had a warm drink. He also wolfed down his sandwiches, trying to remember when he was last this hungry.

All too soon it was time to get back to work, and

Edward was quick to notice the look of concern on Maggie's face as Jacob pushed himself up out of his chair while trying to disguise the difficulty he was having. He must be approaching sixty years of age, thought Edward, and doing such work as this for so long must have taken toll of his joints. The hours were long and the holidays few, he gathered.

A couple of hours later, after moving to the west meadow to deal with brambles, he was suddenly joined by his puffing four-legged companion, followed by Ellen Willmott who was also puffing but trying hard not to show it.

'How are you feeling?' she asked, after catching her breath.

'Aching all over,' he admitted, 'but very content. Everything is as I hoped it would be.'

'So, will we see you tomorrow?' she asked, somewhat anxiously.

'If you'll have me, yes, certainly. And may I bring Rufus again?'

'I would be delighted to see you, and so would Jacob, I'm sure. And yes, of course Rufus can come. He can either stay with you or come to me, I am happy either way. Now I think you have done more than enough for a first day. I suggest you let Jacob know, and go to the comfort of your home. Thank you for what you have done today.'

With that, she turned and made her way to the Alpine Garden and then, he assumed, back to her house.

Edward took Rufus' lead, waved goodbye to Jacob, and started on the short walk home. As he made his way past South Lodge and the Thatchers, he noticed a figure sitting with his back to him. He couldn't see the face, but the black and red kerchief round his neck was familiar.

12

Bats, Logs and Other Things
August 2013

'OK,' said David as they gathered round him in the car park. 'First of all, we have a new volunteer, Chris.'

He waved at a slightly overweight but fit looking man who looked 60 but could have been older, with a mop of white hair and a well-trimmed black beard streaked with grey.

'Never mind,' said Gordon sympathetically.

'First of all,' said David, 'and very importantly, never take any notice of Gordon. It almost certainly won't be true.'

'But the truth is so boring,' explained Gordon.

'This is Ken, Donald, Robert, Anne, Beverley...' He briefly introduced all those standing round.

'You will be tested before you go home,' explained Gordon. 'If you can remember the names of eight out of ten volunteers you can come next week. If you remember all of them then you can't come back because that sort of memory will embarrass the rest of us.'

Chris grinned.

'Our tree man came from HQ over the weekend and lopped the top off the ash tree between posts 5 and 6.'

'Is that the one with honey fungus on the roots?' asked Gordon. 'The one that could have fallen in the road?'

'That's right.'

'Why didn't he chop it down altogether? asked Ken. 'It's obviously dead and it could fall on us, or on visitors.'

'Well unfortunately there is a bat hole high up. The chap that came is not allowed to fell a tree that might have bats living in it.'

'So bats health is more important than us humans?' suggested Robert.

'No, but if we make too much of a fuss then they will close the path and visitors will have to use a different route. The rules on bat preservation are very strict.'

'Well,' said Gordon. 'If they want the bats preserved we could buy some formaldehyde and preserve them ourselves.'

'Can't you look in the hole and see if there are any bats in it?' asked Chris.

'And if there are, a sharp stick might solve the problem,' suggested Gordon.

'I've pointed out to HQ,' said David patiently, 'that the tree is still tall enough that if it falls it could either fall in the road or cause another tree to fall in the road and that would be very dangerous. So someone will probably come back and inspect it and fell it completely. Meanwhile there is a lot of wood to clear up and a bonfire to light.'

Anne promptly fished a load of old newspapers from the boot and she and Beverley walked briskly off to start the bonfire, one of the many jobs on which they had become adept. They ignored Robert and Gordon who were talking about climate change and bonfires rather loudly.

'Have you been round Warley Place before?' David asked Chris.

'Well I came round on one of your open weekends once,' he said, 'and once on my own last week to see a bit more, but I don't know much about it.'

'I hate to say this, but if you can separate fact from fiction it would be a good idea if you go round with Gordon and he can tell you about the history of the place. Look for anything that needs attention, either because it's unsafe or unsightly. Make sure you push the posts to see if they are rotting; take some loppers and secateurs in case anything is hanging across the path. Then let Harry or me know.'

Gordon smiled at Chris and shook hands.

'Oh, and by the way,' said David to Chris. 'Don't forget what I said. If he tells you that you'll have to polish the holly leaves don't believe him. He told one volunteer that and I'm not sure that he ever came back.'

The tree clearing group walked briskly through the gate and up the drive. Gordon and Chris stood in the drive alongside the car park.

'David is very good,' explained Gordon. 'I'm getting on in years, as you can see, so I don't do so much of the heavier work as I used to. He makes sure that no-one does more than they should. That's quite a problem sometimes because every single volunteer puts their heart and soul into the work. I enjoy telling people about Warley Place but I'll try not to bore you.'

'You won't bore me. I want to learn about it. Do those cows belong to Essex Wildlife Trust?' he waved at a dozen cows munching the grass in the meadow.

'No, a grazier brings them in the summer each year. It suits both of us, we get the grass cut and he gets his cows fed. You just have to be careful about stepping on to cow pats but apart from that, and the occasional escape, they don't give us any trouble.'

Chris started to open the gate to go up the drive.

'Hang on a minute,' said Gordon. 'Do you see that cottage by the entrance?'

'Yes, presumably it belongs to the pub. It looks quite old.'

'It actually belongs to the Warley Place estate. The owner of Warley Place leases the pub car park and the cottage to the pub. Ellen Willmott's alpine gardener, Jacob Maurer, lived there once he got married. Before that he lived in a bothy over the road with all the other unmarried staff.'

'Handy for the job then.'

'Oh yes. He had nine children – '

'Nine?!'

'Yes, five girls all named after flowers, and four boys. From what research we have done he was a really nice bloke. Everyone who knew him liked him. And he was very good at his job. Ellen Willmott knew an expert when she saw one, so she enticed him away from Switzerland when he was 19 years old and he spent the whole of his working life here. The alpine garden was really something apparently, admired by all the experts and also royalty.'

They turned and walked slowly up the drive into the reserve.

'When Ellen Willmott died she had no direct descendants and it was left to her brother-in-law, who had enough problems keeping his own estate in Worcester going. Ellen Willmott was broke when she died so after naturally moving a lot of the plants to his estate and keeping a few personal items, he sold the rest. The woman that bought it sold it on to a developer who wanted to turn it in to a housing estate, but that fell through and eventually it was leased to Essex Wildlife Trust to run as a sort of historic garden and nature reserve.'

They collected a pair of loppers and secateurs and carried on along the route shown on the trail guide. Past the Headache Tree, Japanese Paper Mulberry tree, the three rockeries, then to where the cart was now parked. Volunteers were busy sawing up branches and packing the cart ready to take it to the bonfire site.

'Why don't you just leave it as habitat for the animals?' asked Chris.

'Well, there are quite a few habitat piles tucked away out of sight,' explained Gordon. 'Some of the bigger logs will probably be left to rot for insects to live in, and the thinner ones used as path markers, but the smaller branches we've found are best just burnt, or occasionally used to make dry hedges.'

They carried on through the winding path, past the cold frames, the ruins of greenhouses, an old nursery bed and a reservoir beside what used to be the coach house and stables.

'Who is the young chap?' asked Chris. 'Does he have Mondays off work?'

'Oh that's Ken. His father owns a garden centre and Ken now runs a small specialist nursery as part of it not far from here. His wife Elsie comes here too quite a lot but usually one or other of them has to stay there. She's due to have a baby soon so I expect she doesn't want to risk doing too much at the moment.'

After a brief look round the walled garden they turned and went by the currently forlorn-looking daffodil bank, then after passing through a tree-lined stretch Gordon stopped.

'This was her bog garden,' he said, indicating some humps on the left. 'When it rains it fills with water and those humps become islands. But that' he said, indicating a large area devoid of trees and surrounded by a concrete edging, 'was her boating lake. Unlike the bog garden, it doesn't matter how hard it rains, it's always dry.'

'It's huge,' commented Chris. 'How old is it?'

'Well, Ellen Willmott had it built, but we're not sure exactly when. We don't know when it started leaking, either.'

They walked in silence for a while, then turned to go up the hill alongside the west meadow.

'Ellen Willmott seemed to have admired Napoleon in some ways,' commented Gordon.

'This isn't one or your stories David warned me about, is it?' grinned Chris.

'No, honestly. I've seen the list of her books which were auctioned when she died, and there are quite a few about him. Anyway, apparently she bought the hut Napoleon used when crossing the Alps on his way to Milan, had it dismantled and re-erected here by the ponds. There's no sign of it now, though.'

'North pond on our left,' said Gordon, as they passed a bird hide. 'Not much in it now, but it's a nice quiet place to watch the birds.'

The row of Spanish chestnuts then appeared as, somewhat out of breath, they neared the top of the climb.

'Lovely view, isn't it?' said Chris as they gazed out over London. 'I used to work down there. Not in London itself, but the suburbs. I hated travelling even that far.'

'What did you do?'

'I was a teacher.'

'Pretty stressful I'd guess, bearing in mind how some of today's youngsters behave and what little respect they have for authority.'

'That's true, but most of them are great and just want to learn. Now I want to.'

They wandered along the path towards the little bridge over the gorge and stood on it looking at what used to be the alpine garden but was now a dry stream bed lined with huge rocks.

'I always find this a little sad,' whispered Gordon. 'I can imagine poor Jacob slaving away here on these slopes, usually twelve hours a day producing one of the marvels of the Victorian gardening world, Ellen Willmott getting all the credit, and now it's all gone anyway.'

'Do you have any photographs?'

'Not in colour, and very few in black and white.'

Gordon glanced at his watch.

'Did you bring anything to eat? It's tea break now and my rucksack is still in my car.'

'Mine too, and yes, I brought a vacuum of coffee and some biscuits.'

They made their way back to the conservatory via their cars to find most of the volunteers already sitting there.

'Did you remember what I told you about Gordon?' asked David grinning as Gordon and Chris squeezed on to a vacant bench. 'You didn't believe any of it did you?'

'No, of course not,' said Chris. 'Especially the bit about you being such a good warden and how you got the best out of people. Just as well you warned me.'

'Oh God,' groaned David. 'Not another wind-up merchant!'

'I think I'm going to like coming here,' said Chris. 'All this entertainment for free.'

Robert clutched his head and put his hands over his ears. Gordon burst out laughing.

'Robert is our archivist,' he explained. 'But he is also a bit particular about grammar. Isn't that right Robert?'

Robert put his hands down. 'Has he stopped saying 'for free'?'

'But everyone says that,' protested Chris.

'No, that's not true. I don't.'

'Nor me,' said Gordon. 'Wouldn't dream of it.'

'I wouldn't either,' said Ken. 'Knowing the abuse I'd get if I did!'

'You can say 'for nothing' or 'free of charge' or just 'free', because 'free is an adjective. It describes something.'

'OK, so not everyone says it, but most people do and it's in all the newspapers and I've heard it on the television.'

'I know,' said Robert gloomily. 'The cause is lost. But some of us will fight on.'

'I'll try to remember it,' said Chris. 'Me and Gordon went round the reserve – what have I said now?'

Robert had his head in his hands, but took them away and looked up, grinning.

'I'm not totally serious, it's just that that is one of my *bêtes noire*. It's grammatically correct, don't worry, but I always think it's more polite to put the other person first. So you should say 'Gordon and I'. But, again, it seems to be the thing to say these days so I've given up on that one. What were you going to say?'

'I'm frightened to say anything now! I was going to say how peaceful and interesting the place is. Gordon was telling me a bit about the history and I'd like to know more.'

'Robert is certainly the person to talk to,' said Gordon. 'He's got loads of stuff. Pictures from Ellen Willmott's time, old letters, you name it. Just make sure you've got a couple of hours to spare though.'

'At least,' said David.

'You can come round for a delicious cup of coffee and

I'll show you everything,' offered Robert. 'Just give me a ring when you're free.'

'Er, shouldn't that have been 'a cup of delicious coffee?' asked Chris. 'The coffee being delicious, not the cup. A misplaced modifier I think.'

'I... er... what? Yes, I suppose...'

Gordon was laughing so much he had to put his cup down for fear of spilling it.

'I'm a retired teacher,' explained Chris. 'I taught English among other things. Gordon put me up to saying 'for free' and 'me and Gordon'. I happen to agree with you.'

'I knew it was a mistake letting Gordon go round with you,' groaned David.

'Well that's taught me a lesson,' laughed Robert. 'I look forward to that coffee.'

'OK,' said David. 'Anyone else got anything to report.'

'Well,' said Gordon.

'Except Gordon,' said David.

'I won't mention any names for fear of embarrassing Donald,' said Gordon, ignoring David. 'But someone has broken an item of equipment.'

Donald gazed innocently up at the sky.

'All right Donald, what have you done?'

'Well remember that rather expensive pole saw and you said to be sure it was fixed properly, because otherwise the top bit could come out and stay right up in the tree?'

'Oh no!'

'Well it was a good job you reminded me because I remembered to do it and we got the branch down and the saw with it.'

'So the pole saw is OK?'

'Oh yes, it's fine. But you remember you put a new

engine in the tractor and generally did it up so it looked like new.'

'Don't tell me. The branch fell on the tractor.'

'No, it missed it. Not by much, but it was fine. We had to cut the branch up to cart it to the bonfire site. We had a nice new pair of loppers with us.'

'That pair I've just bought in today?! You haven't broken them already?'

'Of course not.' Donald put on an injured expression. 'It's just that we should have used them. I used that old pair of secateurs instead. The ones you were going to throw away. The blade broke. Sorry.'

'Why don't I learn when you two get together?' complained David. 'Back to work. Or in the case of two of you, just 'to work'. There are some fence posts to replace, sycamore seedlings to pull up, leaves to sweep up for the leaf mould bins, bonfire to see to, strimming the crocus area....'

He was well aware of the volunteers' various abilities and allocated the tasks accordingly.

13

Ripples in a Pond
15 August 1934

Edward eased his aching limbs on to one of the rocks overlooking the south pond towards the carriage drive and east meadow beyond. He had previously tried sitting on an old bench in the remains of a gazebo in the corner of the Pleasaunce. Once a pleasing wooden structure under which the Willmott family took tea, it had lost most of its roof and the sides comprised as much fresh air as timber. However it would provide a welcome place to sit and provide some shade from the sun, he thought. Until it collapsed, that is, leaving him sitting in a pile of rotting timber.

Jacob had said several times that he was welcome to take lunch in his cottage, but Edward enjoyed just relaxing in quiet contemplation for half an hour in the company of his dog. For that, this rock suited him admirably. Its shape even permitted him to rest his back, if he wished.

He opened his box and looked at the sandwiches. Cheese again. He liked cheese. He was a vegetarian, but even if he wasn't he thought he would still prefer cheese. They were proper doorsteps, not the delicate offerings that his dear wife used to provide. First taking a long draught of water from his bottle, he then selected one and hungrily bit into the large bread-covered wedge of cheddar. It was delicious.

Savouring each mouthful, saving a corner of each sandwich for the salivating Rufus, he soon found himself looking at the empty box.

The work was very hard, but after a month here he was fitter than he had been for a long time, and more content. Ellen Willmott had not been the demanding taskmaster – or should that be taskmistress, he wondered – that he thought she might have been. In fact she had taken great pleasure in introducing him to the delights of botany, as had Jacob. He did not think there could have been two better teachers in the land. He had no idea that stigmas, styles, ovaries, carpels and a seemingly endless number of other parts of a plant could be so interesting.

However behind the facade of enthusiasm and pride in her garden, he could see that Ellen Willmott was deeply troubled. All around was the evidence of deterioration of what was once arguably the most renowned private garden in the country, packed full of exotic species that others could only dream of. To maintain it in its former glory would have needed a small army of gardeners, and a rolling programme enabling buildings to be maintained and new and replacement plants to be purchased. She could afford neither.

But that was not all that was concerning her. Perhaps she was not even aware of what it was. He was not sure himself.

He was feeling sleepy; the warmth, the sandwiches, the tired muscles, all conspired against a swift return to work.

Then he heard it. A chug chug noise, like his rather worn out old Austin labouring up the hill. But there were now no cars at Warley Place, he was pretty sure of that.

Looking out through the trees and bushes towards the drive he thought he saw something. A strange vehicle

130

with handlebars towing a cart full of logs, disappearing behind the vegetation and then appearing again. A man appeared to be walking alongside guiding the handlebars, and two more walking behind. Indistinct, becoming even more so as he tried to see it more clearly; he had no idea what it was. Some contraption dreamed up by the resourceful owner of Warley Place, he imagined. Rufus, too, was staring into the distance.

'And how are you today?'

The now familiar rather high pitched voice made him jump and he was suddenly fully alert.

'Very well, thank you,' he said getting to his feet. 'I was just wondering what that was.'

'What what was?' asked a puzzled Ellen Willmott.

'That motor device,' said Edward, waving towards the drive, suddenly realising that the only sound he could now hear was the rustling of the leaves and the twittering of birds.

'Probably just a car travelling on the by-pass,' she said, looking at the main road on the far side of the meadow and seeing nothing.

'It must have been,' agreed Edward, knowing that it was no such thing.

'I have been pulling up *Fallopia japonica*,' he continued, changing the subject. 'And also ragwort from the meadow. Both those things seem to grow exceedingly well. Far too well for Jacob's liking!'

'Jacob is correct. They do need to be kept in check, but it is a thankless task, not least because one is continually bending and pulling, a most unnatural action that has an unfortunate effect on one's back.'

'So I have discovered,' said Edward ruefully. 'And if one crouches, it has the same effect on one's knees!'

She laughed.

'Please excuse my familiarity,' said Edward, ' but it is a joy to hear you laugh.'

'It is a joy to do so,' she said. Then, more sadly, 'Since my dear sister Rose and my very good friend Sir Norman Moore died I have laughed little.'

'Who was Norman Moore?' asked Edward.

'Sir Norman..... Oh, I forgot, you people have no truck with titles, do you.'

'You know about Quakers then?'

'A little. I had a herbaceous foreman, Thomas Candler, who had Quaker tendencies.'

She was quiet for a moment.

'He left before the war. I am afraid I did not give him a good testimonial.'

'Why, was he not good at his job?'

'Oh yes, very good. But do not ask me why I could not say so at the time. When he decided to move on I simply could not do so.'

'I apologise, I am intruding into private affairs that are no concern of mine.'

'Dr Moore – you have no objection to the term 'doctor'?'

'I do not have any objection to other people using titles at all. As far as the term 'doctor' is concerned, in my own opinion it is an earned title and one I would be most happy to use.'

'Dr Moore was a close friend of the family, and as well as giving us excellent medical advice from time to time, he was also a close confidant. Someone to whom we could all feel able to reveal our innermost thoughts. A very good friend indeed.'

'May I ask what happened to him?'

'Indeed you may. Sadly, a few years after receiving his

baronetcy, he passed away. He served St Bartholomew's Hospital in many ways, in later years as consulting physician, and wrote *The History of St Bartholomew's Hospital* in his spare time. He also – but I bore you.'

'Not at all. I would like to know more about him when you have the time. But I suppose I should be getting back to work.'

'Which, now I recall, is why I came to find you. Presumably your career means you have some mechanical leanings?'

'Some,' confirmed Edward.

'Some of the window mechanisms in my conservatories are not working as well as they should, and in this weather ventilation is vital. Could you look at them and do what you can?'

'Actually I did look at them yesterday. I noticed that not all of the greenhouses are now in use. Would it be acceptable to you if I used some of the mechanisms on the unused greenhouses? I believe I could make two fully operational greenhouses out of the four grouped together just past the nursery beds.'

'An excellent idea, if that would help.'

She paused for a moment.

'You will have become aware, no doubt, that it is all too much. Too much for me, too much for you and Jacob, and too much for my purse.'

'Yes, I had noticed. But by concentrating on the smallest and best part of your garden we are able to keep it presentable, at least. The weather has not helped, either. Drought last year, winter storms and drought again this year.'

'There were snowstorms and high winds last winter, but the rainfall was less than normal and certainly did not make up the deficit. I am at my wits end.'

To Edward's surprise she lowered herself on to his rock. He pretended not to notice the creaking noise, presumably from her knees, and sat down again himself, though at a respectful distance.

'When I go,' she said, with no trace of self-pity but a sadness in her eyes, 'I wonder how long it will be before all this reverts to wilderness. Will it all have been for nothing?'

'It will be different, no doubt,' said Edward slowly. 'But I know that it will still be loved for many a long year.'

'Different?'

'This garden is you. Owned by someone else it will be different.... wilder.'

'And it will be as if I had never existed.'

Edward looked at two moorhens swimming across the pond, ripples fanning out behind them, spoiling the otherwise glass-like water. Their chicks were swimming to the rear, criss-crossing in search of insects, their own little ripples following them.

'Your life,' he said, 'is like that of a moorhen.'

'Really?' she commented, amused.

'You leave ripples behind, some large, some small. Those ripples react with other ripples – with mine, for instance, and Jacob's, as you can see. I am one of those chicks; Jacob is another. And our ripples will interact with others, and so on.'

He looked at the dancing reflection in the water and saw more clearly.

'The biggest ripple you made is in making Warley Place what it is today. That ripple will change; it is impossible to say how, any more than you or I could make sense of those on the pond in front of us as they follow those little chicks dancing back and forth, leaving an ever changing pattern until they reach the edges of the pond, and even then are reflected from the rocks and bounce back out again.'

'But those ripples will fade away, and the water will become still. What then?'

'What then indeed. Men have long pondered that question.'

A vision of that strange vehicle flashed across his mind.

'Warley Place, like the pond, will be still for a while, responding only to the whims of nature. But the ripples have done their work. Those chicks will thrive and make their own new ripples, and the pond will be alive again, but different from before, I feel.'

'So I am a moorhen, making ripples in a pond?'

'I fear so,' smiled Edward. 'But a big pond, and perhaps making waves more than ripples.'

'When I join my mother and my father my garden will become a wilderness. No-one will want to spend the money as I have done. My brother in law will not want it, he lives too far away.'

Edward looked again into the pond; at the ripples, the reflections, the busy little ducklings.

'When that time comes it may well sink into disrepair but I see people working here, people visiting here, people who will love and treasure what remains of your garden, people who live in harmony with nature. People who will thank you, though you are no longer here.'

'Wishful thinking,' sighed Ellen Willmott. 'And how about you? Are you finding the clearness you desired? Are you content?'

'One can be contented if one reconciles three things,' said Edward. 'What you expect from other people; what other people expect from you; and what you expect from yourself. At the moment I am happy with what you have given me – an opportunity; you do not demand from me more than I can give; and that is all I expect from myself, at the moment. So yes, I am contented. And you?'

'I think you know full well that I am not,' she said, sadly. 'I know that I demand too much from others, poor Jacob in particular, and I take James Robinson very much for granted. We have just been talking about how my life's work is disintegrating around me. I am not at all happy with my own performance. So I fail at every stage of your contentment requirement. I and my garden will be forgotten.'

Edward wondered how he could be so certain that she was wrong.

'Jacob told me about your lovely garden at Tresserve,' Edward said. 'Also, one in Italy. It seems to me that you took on more than any one person could possibly handle. I wish I could have seen them.'

'Yes, they were lovely, both of them,' she said wistfully. 'In fact, when things started to get really hard I contemplated selling Warley Place and moving to France, to stay in Tresserve. But my real love was here, I couldn't just leave it. As it has turned out, though, it would not have made much difference in the long run.'

'Why did you buy the Tresserve estate?'

'One of those ripples you were talking about, I suppose. I suffered from rheumatism even then, and my doctor recommended taking the cure at the baths in Aix-les-Bains. My sister and I stayed in Aix for some time and Tresserve is close by, on the shore of Lac du Bourget, and we both fell in love with the people, the area, and this lovely chateau with a lovely garden demanding to be made even more beautiful.'

'I'm afraid I can visualise it only too well,' laughed Edward, 'and the wish to have done so has disturbed the level of my contentment.'

'Thank you for listening to an old woman's moans,' said Ellen Willmott. 'I rarely get the chance to air them.'

'It is I who should thank you,' said Edward. 'Oh well, back to work.'

They both rose, only to see a figure coming up the path from the drive. A well-dressed middle-aged man, with a broad smile.

'I'm terribly sorry to disturb you,' he said pleasantly, 'I was looking for Miss Willmott to offer my services.'

'I am Miss Willmott, and we do not need any services.'

'Oh no, I didn't explain myself clearly. I am in part time employment, which is adequate for my needs, but I get bored. I do not have a garden of any size and I was at one time fully employed on that work.'

Ellen Willmott said nothing.

'Not that I did anything important,' the visitor said hurriedly. 'Just clearing weeds, doing general repair work, that sort of thing. I would like to work with no need for payment. Perhaps after, say, a month, if you see my worth you may wish to pay a modest wage, but that would be entirely up to you.'

'I'm sure it would,' she said. 'What do you think, Mr Saxon?'

'Well we could do with an extra hand,' Edward said, but he was wondering where he had seen this man before.

'There is a great deal to do,' she said.

'Yes, but with a little extra help it could be brought back to its former glory. Even now I marvel at it when I pass. *Labor omnia vincit.*'

'Hard work conquers all' Ellen Willmott explained to

137

Edward. 'Oh, I'm sorry, you may already have known that.'

'No,' said Edward. 'I never studied Latin.'

'*Ad Meliora*,' said an encouraged Nigel. 'I have often marvelled at the crocuses in your meadow, a veritable sea of purple, *Crocus vernus* I assume. And this road, my dear father used to walk upon it when it was the main road to – '

'Yes, I am aware of what it was And your name sir?'

'Nigel Jackson, madam. I am available whenever you wish.'

'Depending on the requirements of your part time job,' suggested Edward.

'Oh yes, but there is some flexibility with that.'

'Very well then, *Vincere in bono malum*,' said Ellen Willmott.

'Indeed,' said a slightly worried Nigel, wishing he knew more Latin than he did. Perhaps he shouldn't have assumed her ignorance of that language.

'I shall certainly consider your offer,' she continued. 'If you leave your contact details with Mr Maurer at the lodge, I will let you know. *Adiantum pedatum.*'

'And to you madam, thank-you for your time.'

Once he was out of earshot Ellen Willmott turned to Edward.

'What do you think?' she asked.

'There is something about him that doesn't appear genuine,' he said. 'I've seen him somewhere before, but can't remember where. But maybe I am being harsh. But I noticed that you asked him to leave his details with Jacob, rather than your butler.'

Ellen Willmott smiled.

'*Bono malum superate* means 'overcome evil with

good'. What I said, *Vincere in bono malum* means overcome good with evil. He didn't pick it up, so I guessed his Latin was not as good as he would like us to believe. And I did not want to give him an excuse to go to my house to see Robinson. I doubt if he will leave anything with Jacob.'

'And *Adiantum pedatum*?'

'Oh, that's a Maidenhair Fern,' just like the one behind you. If he had queried it, I'd have just said that I wanted his opinion of it. So, his gardening expertise is as suspect as his Latin.'

'My goodness, that was astute of you.'

'One of the reasons I welcomed your presence here, was your complete honesty,' she said. 'As well as your concern for me when that other horrible man was, I am sure, waiting for the right moment to steal my bag.'

'That's it!' exclaimed Edward. 'I saw him sitting at a table with that man, Bertie something or other. I made enquiries and apparently he is a small-time thief, but not known for physical violence, so your bag would have gone but you would probably not have been harmed.'

'This man could have been one of your bigger ripples,' remarked Ellen Willmott. 'But hopefully he was a small ripple that has now died out.'

'I hope so,' said Edward. 'Although we must be vigilant.'

14

Metal Detecting
July 2013

'Elsie, that's a lovely present,' said Ken. 'How did you know I wanted a metal detector?'

'I saw the look in your eye when you mentioned that David had one,' she said, her eyes sparkling at his pleasure. 'We've almost finished clearing the third rockery so there will be a lot more labels to find.'

Although many of Ellen Willmott's original plant labels had gone to Spetchley Park when she died, along with the specimen plants, many more had been unearthed from time to time as rockeries and other areas were cleared. Most of them had been cast oval labels on long iron stalks, but quite a few had been what looked like thin zinc, with either stamped or handwritten names on them. It was amazing that many of the handwritten ones were as clear as the day they were written, although others had suffered from corrosion and were hard to decipher.

'Wow, this is a really good one,' said Ken as he looked at the panel with various buttons and lights. 'Ground Balance, Discrimination, Pinpoint... I hope there's a manual with it!'

'Ground Balance is to allow for the minerals in the soil,' explained Elsie. 'Discrimination is so that you can detect different metals instead of all of them, and Pinpoint is when you want to find out exactly where something is.'

Ken just stood there with his mouth open.

'I got some advice from David,' she laughed.

'I think I'll do the same,' said Ken. 'I'm going to have fun with this. Anne is keeping a list of all the labels so it will keep her busy too.'

'Yes, she said she's got over a thousand so far, lots of them with names she's never heard of, so I certainly won't know what they are.'

'I expect I'll detect lots of old iron, tin cans, things like that and very few labels. But I'll enjoy trying it. Perhaps we can do it together?'

'That would be nice.'

'Yes, I could do the detecting and you could do the digging,' he continued, dodging a swipe from his wife.

'It's Wednesday, isn't it. I think Anne and Harry will be finishing off clearing the rockery. And David should be there too to give us some tips. We could do it then. I'll ask Dad if he'll look after the nursery for us.'

'Don't forget we're going there in the evening for a birthday drink,' she reminded him.

'I'll just have a look at the instructions though,' said Ken, opening up the leaflet.

'Breakfast first,' she said. 'I'm not sure if marmalade or milk would do the detector much good. There's plenty of time, so don't gulp it down.'

She popped the toast in the toaster while he poured milk over his cereal, placing the instructions alongside the bowl.

'Actually you could use the detector, I'll do the digging,' he said. 'Just in case.'

'I'm not ill or delicate,' she reminded him. 'I'm just pregnant. I can do ....'

Suddenly she stopped and put her hand to her stomach.

'Not well?' he asked anxiously. 'I thought your

141

morning sickness had gone. We'd better see the doctor. What are you smiling for?'

'It's only kicking again,' she said.

She grabbed his hand and held it to her stomach.

'Oh yes. It's strange to think of it moving away in there. You OK?'

'Yes. I'm so happy.'

He gently wiped the tears away from her cheeks.

* * *

Ken opened the tailgate to get their boots out.

'I see Anne and David have beaten us to it,' he commented. 'I expect Harry will be here soon. We'll go up and get started.'

David was concerned about health and safety and always made sure they wore steel toe-capped boots and gloves even for normal 'gardening' work so they sat on the back of the car and pulled on socks and boots. Elsie put her little camera and sketchbook in her bag along with trowel, water and muesli bar. Ken grabbed his rucksack and detector, locked the car, and they made their way through the gate and up the drive to the rockeries.

The grass was getting long in the meadow, but the cows would be arriving soon and would deal with that. Before they did, thistles would need to be strimmed and ragwort pulled, but that would be a Monday job.

'July always seems a sort of in-between month here,' Ken said, looking around as they walked past the now colourless rhododendrons. 'The spring colour has gone and we're waiting for the autumn.'

'I was thinking that too,' said Elsie. 'I expect it would have been different in Ellen Willmott's time.'

'There's usually more insects now though. Hoverflies and bees, but lots of interesting creepy crawlies.'

Passing the old turning circle with its display of thistles, they saw Anne through the trees working on one of the rockeries and made their way through.

'Hi Anne.'

She turned, startled.

'Sorry, I was miles away. Hi Elsie, good to see you. You don't normally come on a Wednesday, do you?'

'No, but it's my birthday,' said Ken.

'Even more reason to stay at home.'

'No, I thought I'd come for my present and to eat my birthday cake. Where is it?'

'You'll be lucky. There's a barrow, there's a spade.'

'You haven't asked me what this is.'

'Whatever it is it doesn't look much good for digging with. All right, you are dying to tell me. What is it.'

'It's a metal detector. Elsie bought it for me. She said it would be good for finding plant labels and that I could do the detecting and you could dig the holes.'

'You liar!' laughed Elsie. 'You know someone is going to believe one of your remarks one of these days and then you'll be sorry!'

'It's OK Elsie,' said Anne. 'It's more likely to be the other way round. One day he'll be telling the truth and no-one will believe him and he'll wonder why.'

'Oh well,' he grumbled. 'I suppose I'd better get on with it.'

'Causing disruption as usual?' asked Harry, dropping his rucksack by the tree in the middle of the rockery.

'What else do you expect?' said Anne, getting back to her digging.

'Whose metal detector is this?' asked Harry.

'Mine, a birthday present from Elsie,' said Ken. 'Why don't you try it out Elsie? The instructions are in my bag.'

'No, you should use it first, it's your present.'

'I'll get told off if I stop digging, you work it all out then you can explain it all to me.'

'I was going to help with clearing the rockery.'

'Please?'

'Go on Elsie,' said Anne. 'We'd like to know if there is anything here.'

They carried on digging, exposing a stone path, to the accompaniment of various bleeps and whines until they stopped for a break.

'Blimey, this is hard on your back isn't it,' said Harry.

'The rockery seems to have collapsed,' said Ken. 'Perhaps the rabbits burrowed under them. It will need a trowel and a brush for this bit. Have you got the detector working yet Elsie?'

'I think so,' she said, putting her sketch pad down and passing the detector to him.

'Press that button to turn it on.'

He did so and it played what sounded like a short tune.

'Those different notes are for the different metals it detects. But I've left it set to detect everything, including iron. You have to sweep it from side to side because it only picks a signal when it's moving. There's another setting for pinpointing where things are but I'm not sure how that works.'

Ken moved the head over the ground and soon got a bleep; Anne started to dig and her spade struck something hard.

'There's definitely something there,' she said, grabbing her trowel and clearing round it. She was soon triumphantly producing a rusty old bit of pipe.

'I shall clean it up and get it mounted with a little label to remember my very first find,' he said. 'Here you are Elsie, you have a go.'

He passed the device to her and they watched while she scanned a little further on until there was another bleep. Ken got his spade and dug a big clod of earth out and looked in the hole. Elsie scanned the hole and it still bleeped, so they knew it was not in the clod that had been removed. Ken knelt down with his trowel and scraped away some more earth.

'I can see it,' he said, 'it's just poking out of the side of the hole.'

Retrieving his spade he widened the hole a bit, then reaching down he slowly pulled out a long spike of iron with an oval welded to the top. Anne produced a scrubbing brush and Ken cleaned the oval bit. As had been the case with so many other labels, it was perfectly clear.

' It says "I. kochii", *Iris kochii*,' he said.

'Well done Elsie,' said Anne. 'Perhaps you could teach Ken how to find labels rather than bits of pipe?'

'OK, OK,' said Ken. 'I'll have another go. Any idea what an *Iris kochii* is? And don't say it's an Iris, I got that far myself.'

'I think it's one of the purple bearded irises, but I don't know what 'kochi' means. It might be a place or a person, I don't think it relates to the plant itself.'

He gave the label to Anne for her collection and carried on from where Elsie had finished and after a couple of false alarms he found a good signal and picked his spade up again. He dug a big clod out as before, then took his trowel.

'I don't want to run the spade through anything important,' he explained.

He soon found something and carefully exposed a long flat piece of metal.

'Hello, what have you got here, a metal detector I see,' said a new voice. David had appeared, taking a break from strimming nettles.

'Yes,' said Ken getting to his feet. 'Elsie found an Iris label and I think I've found one too but it's a strange shape. Pointed at one end, look…'

He handed the mud-encrusted object to David, who scraped some mud off before borrowing Anne's brush.

'Just scrap metal I suppose,' said Ken ruefully.

'No,' replied David, 'but not a label. It's a knife. Or I do believe it's a bayonet. Warley Barracks was just down the road so they might have done manoeuvres here after Ellen Willmott died. They wouldn't have come while she was still alive. Can I take it home and look in my books?'

'You can keep it,' said Ken. 'I don't think I want a bayonet at home. What on earth would a bayonet be doing here?'

'Perhaps the army was doing manoeuvres here during the war,' suggested David. 'I'll try to identify it more precisely and if it is what I think it is, I'll contact the museum at Chelmsford and ask if they want it. If they don't, we'll put it with the other bits and pieces we've dug up.'

'Ken dug up a rather nice piece of old pipe,' Harry said. 'I expect you'd like that too.'

David laughed. 'I've dug a few of those up myself,' he said. 'I think they were part of the arbours that went over the paths. Are you OK Elsie, when's the baby due?'

'I'm fine, a couple of months yet.'

'Do you know if it's a boy or a girl?' asked Anne.

'No,' said Elsie. 'We decided not to know, although people are asking so they can buy a suitable present.'

'I expect you'd like a girl, and Ken would like a boy,' Harry suggested.

'We really don't mind,' said Else.

'No, we don't,' agreed Ken. 'we would love it either way. Although if I had to choose it would be for a daughter. And then a son later.'

'Have you got a name ready if it is a girl?' asked Anne.

'We discussed naming her after one of our mothers, but that might disappoint the other one. Then I wondered about calling her Ellen after Ellen Willmott and we might just do that, but it's a bit, well, obvious. I quite like Laura.'

'I know,' said Harry. 'Make her initials LN, that sounds like Ellen and you can call her that later on if she doesn't like Laura. Laura Nancy, what about that?'

'That's sort of OK but it doesn't roll off the tongue very well,' Ken commented.

'Well Laura Norah then, that rolls off the tongue nicely,' suggested Harry with a grin.

'Just stick to digging Harry,' said Ken, putting the detector away. They continued their digging until an hour later he looked at his watch.

'We'd better go Elsie,' he said. 'I expect Dad will need relieving at the nursery and we'll be getting round to his place early this evening.'

He picked up Elsie's sketch pad and burst out laughing.

'Come and look at this,' he called to the others, ignoring Elsie's protestations.

They joined him in laughing at the full page sketch which showed a recognizable Ken standing on the rise at the middle of the rockery, triumphantly waving a piece of pipe in one hand and a metal detector in the other.

'Oh you must frame that,' said David.

Ken was still chuckling as they packed up their things

and made their way back to the car park, leaving the others to clear a few more metres of the rockery.

Ken looked across at the shed as they sat on the car and took their boots off.

'Remember that?' he said. 'You crawling in there to rescue Gordon? I've never been so scared in my life. I thought you'd be killed along with him. He'll never forget what you did, and nor will I.'

They looked round at the sound of Anne coming through the gate.

'I'll just pop the label in the shed,' she said walking across to it with her key.

Elsie smiled as she saw Ken stop lacing his trainers and his hands clench, re-living that fateful day no doubt.

'Funny really,' she said. 'Ever since I came to Warley Place everything has worked out. Most of all meeting you. It's almost as if it were meant to be. My life would have been so very different otherwise. That scares me more than the shed does.'

'Me too. I've never been happier.'

15

Howard comes home on leave
August 1934

'It's good to see you, Howard,' said Edward as he opened the door and saw his smiling son standing there. He stood aside to let him in. 'My goodness, that uniform really does suit you. Especially those wings above your pocket. Oh dear, if my Quaker friends were here, they would be horrified, but I am still proud of you. Sorry, you are tired after your long journey and I am rabbiting on. Go and get changed into something more comfortable while I prepare some food, you must be famished.'

A big hairy head appeared round the sitting room door, followed by a big hairy body as Rufus condescended to welcome his long-lost friend.'

'Hello Rufus,' Howard said, ruffling the hound's head. 'A cup of tea would go down nicely, father, but nothing to eat yet, thank you. I had lunch on the train and really just want to stretch my legs. How about a walk round this great garden you keep going on about in your letters? If you don't mind going to your place of work during time off?'

'No, that would be fine. I'll get changed.'

'Wait,' said Edward, frowning a little. 'I know this sounds silly, and perhaps it is, but would you consider keeping your uniform on after all?'

'No, I don't mind, but why?'

'It's probably just my imagination, but several times

when aeroplanes have flown over, she has looked wistful, as if she is remembering something – or someone. I wondered if she might like to talk about it. No, I'm being silly, forget it. She might not even be there.'

'She?'

'Sorry, Miss Ellen Willmott.'

'Do you fancy her, then?''

'Oh dear no,' Edward said hurriedly. 'She's much older than I am, and a very formidable lady. No, it's just that sometimes there is a sadness about her. I can't quite fathom it out.'

'It's all right father, I know who she is,' laughed Howard, 'I've seen her about often enough. And I've always wondered what the garden is like on the inside – all I've seen from the road are fields full of purple crocuses and brilliant yellow daffodils. I would be proud to walk with you in my uniform. I'll just dump my bag and freshen up while the tea brews.'

It was so good to have Howard home again. Edward still couldn't reconcile his own views with the need even to prepare for war, but could not find fault with his son's decision after his honest and heartfelt appraisal. The idea of him shooting at, aiming to kill, another human being, appalled him. But the idea of someone like that Adolph Hitler chap, unlikely as it was, starting another war and Britain standing by was equally unacceptable.

'In your letters you said you are flying a Bristol Bulldog,' he said to his son as he reappeared.

Howard sat at the kitchen table and lifted a hot cup to his lips, sipping at it carefully.

'That's nice,' he said. 'Yes, the Bulldog is a great aeroplane. Very manoeuvrable, fast, over 200 miles an hour, and can get up to 30,000 feet – higher than Mount Everest.'

'Biscuit?' asked Edward.

'No, thank you.'

'I think Rufus would like you to reconsider that answer,' laughed Edward. 'But be careful you don't get saliva over those pristine trousers.' He passed Howard a clean tea towel to put on his lap.

'So that means you can dive down to shoot at an enemy aircraft below you, I suppose,' Edward continued.

'Yes, it does. But apart from any tactical advantage, the feeling of being up there, high above the earth, twisting and turning, diving and climbing, looping the loop, it's a tremendous feeling, father.'

'That aircraft that won the Schneider Trophy for us, several years ago I think, that could go at 400 miles an hour and it had great big floats underneath. If the enemy had something like that you wouldn't stand a chance.'

'Oh yes, the Supermarine S.6B. Well, I wouldn't mind betting that the company is already designing a fighter based on that aircraft, and that it will see off anything the enemy can throw at us. Anyway, enough of aeroplanes.' He gulped down the last of his tea and passed most of his biscuit to Rufus who gulped it down before Howard had even taken his hand away. 'I'm dying to stretch my legs and see this fancy woman of yours.' He grinned as his father opened his mouth to protest. 'Only kidding. But I am looking forward to seeing the garden.'

Edward lifted the dog's lead down from a hook, along with the small bag that he always carried in case he had to clear up after Rufus, although this was rarely the case as he had been trained to go in their own garden.

'It's a little run-down in places,' warned Edward as they walked up the slope towards the centre of Great Warley. 'You wouldn't believe it from talking to her, but she's broke, and has been for years.'

151

'I know she dresses a bit strangely, but I thought she was rich.'

'She was, at one time. Her parents left her and her sister pretty well off, and her mother's cousin was very rich and left them a great deal more. As is often the case when folk are given money, they tend to spend it without sufficient thought for the future. Perhaps they imagine they will be given some more. She spent it on buying more property, some in France and in Italy, and in improving her garden. The property seems to have all gone and she has few staff left to tend her plants.'

'Didn't her sister marry into a posh family?'

'Yes, the Berkeley family, a very old and well-established family in Worcestershire. But, sadly, the sister, Rose, died and it almost broke Ellen's heart. They were very close.'

They walked on in silence for a while, until the Thatchers public house came into sight and, beside it, South Lodge, Jacob Maurer's cottage – and a rather forbidding five-bar gate across the driveway.

'Before we go in,' said Edward as he put his hand on the gate, 'just be careful what you say. She could be hiding behind any bush. She's one of those people who knows how to be at the right place at the right time.'

'Seen from her perspective, you mean?' said Howard. 'The wrong place at the wrong time, from the victim's perspective.'

'Oh, yes.'

'Shouldn't you have asked her first?' suggested Howard. 'About showing me round, I mean.'

'Well I did mention that you were coming home on leave for a few days, and I did sort of ask.'

'That's OK then. And she agreed?'

'Well, sort of. I'm sure it will be all right.'

'You don't look too certain about that,' laughed Howard.

'Come on, we'll go to the house before looking at the gardens,' said Edward, closing the gate behind him.

They walked past Jacob's cottage and its propagating houses, various beds and hundreds of plants in an assortment of pots. A little further on was the pond, around and adjacent to which was an alpine garden constructed of huge rocks, and a ravine running through it, plants of all sizes and colours, and beautiful shrubs.

As they left the pond behind, Edward suddenly stopped.

'What is it?' asked Howard.

'My early warning system,' said Edward.

'Your what?'

Edward pointed at Rufus, who was looking up the slope to the left, his tail moving slowly from side to side.

'Who is that?' came a rather strident female voice.

'It is me, Edward,' he called. 'I was looking for you to ask if I could introduce my son to you.'

A large wide-brimmed hat appeared first, moving across a large shrub, until a jumble of clothes, tied together with a rope round the middle, also came into sight. Somewhere between the hat and the clothes a face gradually emerged as the whole collection emerged from the shadows.

'Let him go,' commanded the figure.

Edward released Rufus, who bounded up the slope to get his ears ruffled and his fur stroked.

'Should we come up?' called Edward.

'You may,' came the answer.

They both climbed up the steps, while the figure resumed work with a trowel, and stood there for a moment while she made them wait for the obligatory minute or so.

'That will do, I think,' she said, straightening up and turning to look at them: or rather at Howard. She seemed almost to be in a trance, looking into the distant past, almost unaware of their presence.

'I hope you will forgive me, coming unannounced like this,' said Howard, easily. 'I had heard so much about your wonderful garden, and walked past it so many times. It was a rather selfish to take advantage of my father working here.'

She jerked back to the present.

'No, your father mentioned that you would like to see the garden, you are most welcome. You reminded me of someone else, many years ago; he also was a pilot in the Royal Air Force.'

'A pleasant memory, I hope.'

'Yes, but I had not expected you to be in the Royal Air Force.'

'Why not?'

'Well, bearing in mind your father's beliefs, and perhaps your own. But maybe I shouldn't be surprised at all, bearing in mind Bertie Cadbury.'

'Ah, yes,' said Edward in response to Howard's puzzled look. 'I think I may not have mentioned him.'

Ellen Willmott gave a rather mischievous smile.

'How does not mentioning something fit in with Quaker beliefs?' she asked.

'Not very well,' Edward admitted, then turning to Howard, he explained. 'You know of the Quaker chocolate families, of course.'

'Yes, of course, Cadbury, Fry, Rowntree, and of course the Bourneville village.'

'George Cadbury really lived his faith. During the war one of his sons, Laurence, joined the Friends Ambulance Unit.'

'Yes, I know about the FAU, and how you served in it,' said Howard. 'They were very brave, but then there were a lot of brave people in the war.'

'But his other son, Egbert – Bertie – joined the Royal Navy and later transferred to the air force. He shot down two Zeppelins, the last one in August 1918 being part of the last airship raid on Great Britain. He was horrified to see it, a mass of flames, plunging to earth.'

'I didn't know that,' said Howard, his brow furrowed and his eyes wide open.

'And didn't he receive the Distinguished Flying Cross?' suggested Ellen Willmott.

'Yes, he did, and well deserved it was,' said Edward. 'I suppose I should have reminded you of this, Howard, but I didn't want to encourage you to take up arms.'

'The decision would have been mine anyway,' said Howard. 'Don't let it concern you.'

'Just don't take any unnecessary risks,' said Ellen Willmott earnestly. 'Please.'

'I won't.'

'Anyway, so you've come to look at my garden?'

'If we may, I'd be grateful. I've heard so much about it from my father.'

She looked suspiciously at Edward.

'All good,' said Howard hastily. 'You have some very rare and interesting plants, I gather.'

'Do you know much about gardening?'

'Not a great deal, but I do like finding out about new things, even if I'm not actively involved in their care. Just looking about me here, I can only wonder at the design and construction of this – well, I was going to say rockery, but it's so much more than that. It looks as though it was transported from the Alps.'

'I designed it myself,' said Ellen Willmott, not quite succeeding in preventing her lips from stretching into a smile of satisfaction. 'It's my Alpine garden. Come, I will show you round.'

'If you have the time, that would be very kind of you,' said Howard. 'But before you do, I'm afraid I have to say that I find most of those Latin names very confusing.'

'Me too,' she said. 'It's almost entirely men who name them, so it's not surprising some plants end up with several different names.'

They moved along to a bridge across a gorge cut into the ground, over what looked like a dried-up stream leading down to a pond, its banks composed of huge boulders between which the water must once have flowed.

'That's a strange place to have a greenhouse, if you don't mind my saying so,' commented Howard, pointing at a glass roof across a side channel.

'It's not exactly a greenhouse. It's my filmy fern cave. The roof keeps it warm, while allowing light in, but also maintains the right humidity. And a filmy fern is one in which the fronds are such that one can see through them, like a film.'

'Ah. My father did tell me that you grow plants that others can't, by replicating the conditions in which they originally grew. Now I can see what he meant. You designed all this in order to make sure your alpine plants survived? No, not just survived, flourished.'

'That is correct. Although it is rather late in the year to see its full beauty.'

'I can imagine it. Are those crocuses? I thought they came out in the spring.'

He indicated a large patch of flowers with silvery lilac-blue flowers, leading to a white throat.

'There are autumn crocuses too. They are *Crocus speciosus*.'

'And those, the long spikey things with those little pinkish flowers all the way up?'

'They are *Scilla japonica*. But come on, Mr Saxon, you don't really want to know the names, do you?'

'Well, yes and no. I am interested in them, but admit that I shall have forgotten them by the time we turn the next corner. I shall just admire them in their anonymity. But look, you are very busy. I'm happy to wander round with my father, and leave you to get on with your work.'

'No, I should be glad to accompany you. I get neither opportunity nor satisfaction in walking round on my own. And I would like to hear of your exploits, everyone else talks of nothing but plants. Except your father, of course, but he is always so careful not to offend me it makes me wonder what he really is thinking.'

She turned round to Edward, to see that Jacob had appeared.

'I heard the voices,' he said nervously, 'and wondered whether you needed me to show our visitor round.'

'No thank you Jacob, I can manage. It's time for your break, why don't you have a glass of that blackberry wine of yours with Mr Saxon?'

'Thank you, madam,' he said, looking not a little puzzled.

'He will now say to your father that he cannot understand,' she said, as they walked on over the little bridge. 'I don't normally let him go back to his cottage for his break. Look now.'

157

They both turned and saw Jacob saying something to Edward, then appearing embarrassed as he saw them looking.

'You can come if you wish,' she said to Rufus as the dog followed them.

'There's something magical about this place,' said Howard. 'I don't know what it is. The flowers, the shrubs, the trees, they are wonderful, yes, but it's more than that. There is peace, but tinged with sadness. Not misery, not that sort of sadness, but perhaps a wish for what might have been. No, a wondering at what the future will bring.'

'You are right,' she said, not taking offence. 'I do wonder sometimes if this estate will go untended in the years to come and revert to wilderness. The Berkeley family may help, but they have enough to do with their own estate. My sister married into their family,' she explained. 'She had her own lovely garden there at Spetchley Park, and let me help her sometimes. It's still beautiful and well looked after, but she died some time ago so was unable to appreciate it for as long as we had hoped.'

'Spetchley Park? Where is that?'

'Close to Worcester, a little to the east.'

'We do navigation exercises sometimes, so I must include it in my waypoints and have a look some time.'

'Have you flown over Warley Place?'

'No, but I must do that too. Its real beauty is down here though' then, quickly, 'Oh, no, I didn't mean, well actually...'

Ellen Willmott laughed.

'I do believe you are blushing Mr Saxon! Don't worry, I know exactly what you meant.'

They stopped to look over the west meadow to London, shrouded in mist, before moving on.

'That is a Persian Ironwood tree,' see said, indicating a tree of no great size on their left.

'How strange,' said Howard. 'The branches seem to go in random directions. And they fuse together when they cross. It's a real maverick, isn't it? I assume from the name that the wood is very hard?'

'It is hard, yes. And you are very observant, most people miss its idiosyncrasies. It was very rare when I planted it, brought back to England by Wilson. There are a few more about now, but none as old as mine. Beyond, just this side of that small bank, was where we used to play tennis, or croquet. We haven't done so for many years, though.'

'Is there a bonfire?' asked Howard, as Rufus looked through the trees towards the Pleasaunce. 'I thought I could smell smoke.'

'No, no bonfire,' she said. 'But I too smell smoke sometimes, and occasionally imagine the noise of crackling as wood burns. I also hear the rattle of a cart we do not have. I thought I was losing my mind, but Jacob has heard it too.'

'A haunted garden!' said Howard.

'Haunted maybe, but if so, by a benevolent ghost,' she said. 'Now tell me a little more about what it's like to be up there in the clouds…'

16

Dinner at the Bradshaw's
August 2013

'Don't worry,' said Ken, as for the umpteenth time Elsie asked him if she looked all right. 'We're only going for a relaxing evening meal with mum and dad. We've been married for two years now and you know them well enough to be able to be yourself in their company.'

'Yes, but – '

'No buts.'

'But your mum always does things so nicely.'

'By 'nicely' you mean 'precisely' I suppose. Everything in the right place and done the right way.'

'Well, that too. I just haven't been brought up to worry about some of the things your mum thinks are important. Well, actually, she's right, they <u>are</u> important if we go out to formal dinner. She's never made me feel embarrassed, but I really would like to know how to do things properly.'

'Just relax and be yourself. I married you for what you are, not to be a clone of my mother, much though I love her too. And you really do look lovely. Being pregnant suits you.'

'You liar,' she laughed, looking down at her bulge.

'No, I'm not lying. Come on, get your coat.'

'OK, I'll drive, then you can have a drink.'

'Are you sure you're up to it?'

'Yes, I'm sure. We could walk, but it might be late when we leave and showers are forecast.'

Ken had been somewhat taken aback at how easily Elsie had taken to driving, and a little miffed as well as pleased, when she passed her test first time. He had got through only at the second attempt. But it had proved to be very useful, and a boost to her self-confidence, so he was pleased for himself as well as for her. He grabbed his anorak, and Elsie a deep blue coat that no longer quite met round her expanded midriff.

'I'll drive there, you can drive back,' he said. 'I don't mind your driving when I've had a few drinks to relax me...'

'You could easily end up walking back,' she warned him as she picked her bag up and made for the door.

They climbed in to the rather worn looking Focus estate, Ken's father's old car, and a few minutes later Ken eased it up the drive in front of his parents' house.

'Now just relax,' he said. 'It will be fine.'

The front door opened just before they reached it.

'Come on in,' welcomed a beaming Mrs Bradshaw. 'Let me take your coat Elsie.'

'Sex Discrimination Act 1975,' muttered Ken in a loud whisper.'

'What?'

'It's OK, I won't tell anyone. I'll just hang my own coat up.'

'It's one of the crosses us men have to bear,' said his father sadly, poking his head round the lounge door. 'Best just to get used to it. Hello Elsie, good to see you as usual, but you are looking particularly lovely this evening.'

'Thank you,' said Elsie, blushing. 'My goodness that smells good, I hope you haven't gone to too much trouble for us.' She also hoped there wasn't too much put on her plate. People kept saying she was having to eat for two, but she just couldn't face it.

'I know you might not be able to eat a lot,' said Mrs Bradshaw, as if she could read Elsie's mind. 'I know I couldn't, when I was waiting for Kenneth to arrive. So I've done a risotto, that way you can take as little or as much as you want. Everything is ready, so we might as well go straight in to the dining room.'

Mr Bradshaw ushered Elsie through the door, where she was taken back and not a little frightened by the glistening white table cloth and arrays of cutlery, side plates, glasses, cruet sets, napkins, wine bottles, butter, rolls and goodness knows what else.

'Don't worry,' he whispered as he showed her to her seat, seeing her hesitation and sensing her unease. 'Do as I do.'

Ken sat next to her, and Mr and Mrs Bradshaw opposite, leaving the ends of the table unoccupied. In the middle of the table, on a hotplate, was a large bowl of delicious looking chicken risotto.

Mr Bradshaw uncorked a bottle of white wine and poured some in Ken's glass, then Mrs Bradshaw's and his own.

'I do apologise Elsie,' he said. 'I should have asked you first. I know you aren't drinking alcohol, but would you like some water, a soft drink, lemonade –'

'Oh, I'd love a glass of lemonade,' she said, and waited in silence while he fetched a bottle from the refrigerator and filled her glass.'

'Now, before we start,' said Mrs Bradshaw.

'Oh no,' thought Elsie. 'Please don't ask me to say grace.'

'.... I know it's awkward for you Elsie, not knowing what to call me. "Mrs Bradshaw" is much too formal. I'm not really your mum, although I don't mind you calling me that. But "Stella" sounds much more friendly, and if you can bring yourself to, I'd love you to call me that. I should have insisted ages ago.'

'Oh, thanks Mrs... I mean Stella. I'll do that.'

'And I'm Steve,' said Ken's father. 'Or Stephen, although that's usually reserved for use when 'she who must be obeyed' tells me off!'

Elsie laughed. 'You do make me feel so much at home,' she said. 'I'm so lucky, with Ken of course, but also with you.'

Then, with a couple of lines appearing on her forehead,

'You know my background. Eating fish and chips while watching the television is the sort of thing I have been used to. I get frightened when I go with Ken to a posh restaurant, and a formal meal with a lot of strangers would petrify me.'

'It's easy, once you get used to it. But would you like us to take you through the elements of etiquette tonight?' asked Stella, whose opinion of Elsie rose a couple of notches, recognising the courage it must have taken for her to come out with that admission.

'Oh yes, please,' said Elsie, the crimson fading from her face.

'Best if we do it as we go along?' suggested Steve. 'I'm starving!'

'Yes dear. But first, Elsie, you'll see that the glasses are all on the right, and the side plates for bread are on the left. Remembering that will avoid you eating someone else's roll, as I remember someone once did...'

She looked at Ken, who's innocent eyes were directed at the ceiling.

'The table napkin is either placed on your plate, as I've done, or to your left. Some sources say it's not good etiquette to place it on your lap. That just announces that you are going to spill food there. It's really just to allow you to delicately wipe food from your lips. Others say that you should put it on your lap and only take it off to wipe your mouth. I don't think it matters.'

Elsie noticed Ken start to slip his napkin from his lap, then slipping it back again.

'In a good restaurant you will only have the utensils that you need, and you'll work your way in from the outside. We haven't got knives today, because we are eating risotto, but the knife would be on the right, with its cutting edge facing the plate.'

'I didn't know that,' said Steve. 'Any idea why?'

'No, none at all,' said Stella. Some of the rules make sense, but others don't – although perhaps they did in the old days.'

'What do I do about the roll?' asked Ken. 'I never know whether to break it up, butter it all, or what.'

'You should break it up,' said Stella. 'Take a slab of butter and put it on your bread plate, then using your own butter knife, butter each piece of bread as you eat it – not all at once.'

'Can we start now?' pleaded Steve.

'One more thing.'

Steve groaned. 'Pay attention Elsie,' he warned. 'You will be questioned on this afterwards!'

'Stephen! Normally the host sits at the end of the table. We're not doing it because we wanted a nice relaxed meal. But to be strictly correct you should always wait until the host starts to eat before you do. Unless he or she says otherwise, that is. So Steve is showing good manners for once by not starting, although moaning about it is not considered good etiquette!'

'Shall I serve?' asked Steve.

He picked up the large serving spoon and ladled two spoonfuls on to Elsie's plate.

'Is that sufficient?' he said. 'I'll consult the oracle to find out if it's etiquette to ask for more later.'

'That's fine,' she laughed. 'But I have a feeling I will like a bit more later.'

Once their plates were laden, Ken and Steve picked up their utensils and froze in position, looking at Stella, waiting for her to eat so they could start.

'Oh, all right,' she said, 'you can start now.'

'Hang on a minute,' said Elsie. 'Ken's got a fork in his hand, Steve's got a spoon. I don't know which one to copy!'

Stella laughed.

'I think there are various rules about eating risotto,' she said. 'I hate the American habit of eating food by transferring the fork from the left to the right hand. You can see them chasing peas round the plate. In our case, the spoon is on the right, and it is easier to use it to eat rice with than using a fork. So I'd say, use the spoon. If you do want to use the fork, leave it in the left hand.'

'That's obvious,' said Ken, grinning. 'It leaves the right hand free to use the remote control for the television.'

Stella groaned and put her head in her hands. Elsie picked up her spoon.

'..... and the peas problem is easily overcome, if you have any,' continued Ken. 'There is a poem I've heard, to remind you.'

He put on his most serious face:

'I eat peas with honey;
I've done it all my life.
It does taste rather funny,
But it sticks them to the knife.'

'Spike Milligan,' he explained. 'That well known etiquettist.'

'I was really enjoying this evening up to then,' said Elsie, keeping her face straight and breaking her roll, putting a large pat of butter on her plate. Then, taking a mouthful of risotto, 'But the food is delicious.'

Then they all heard her phone ring, inside her bag.

'Oh no,' she gasped. 'Sorry.'

She reached in grabbed her phone and pushed the 'Off' button, then shoved it back in her bag.

'Well done, Elsie,' said Stella. 'A lot of people would have at least looked to see who was calling and then many would have answered it, even to say where they were. Few would have done what you did, and just turned it off. Obviously, it's good to turn it off beforehand, but we all forget that, from time to time.'

'What should you do if a guest does something wrong, like eating with the wrong utensils?' asked Ken.

'I know the answer to that one,' said Steve. 'There is one golden rule of etiquette. That is, not to embarrass any guest – or the host, of course. So you don't do anything. You just let him get on with it. If he then doesn't have the right utensils to finish his meal, the waiter will quietly provide him with a replacement.'

'And I suppose if he eats your roll,' said Ken, 'you don't say anything, you just reach across over his plate and take his roll.'

'Hmmnnn.... I'll have to think about that one,' said Stella.

'I say, this wine is good,' said Ken. 'Where did you get it? Was it expensive? Whoops, sorry, not very good etiquette, I know. But I'd like to know where to get some from.'

'From my wine club,' said Steve. 'I'll get you a bottle.'

'How do you know whether to have red or white wine?' asked Elsie. 'I've heard it's red with meat, white with fish, is that true? Only I don't like red wine.'

'It used to be the case,' said Steve. 'Certainly, with red meat you'd normally have red wine. With risotto you could have either. But it's just a question of taste. Connoisseurs say red wine tastes better with red meat, but if you don't like red wine, then it's fine to ask for white.'

'If I ask for a little more risotto, you're not going to do your Dickensian Workhouse Master's impression and shout 'MORE?!' are you?' she said to Ken.

'Oh well, I'll restrain myself in this instance,' he said reluctantly.

'I'm glad you like it,' said Stella. 'Just help yourself.'

Elsie ladled another large spoonful of risotto on to her plate, and Ken did likewise, closely followed by Steve.

'We've been looking a bit more into the old plants that Ellen Willmott used to grow,' Ken said, looking at his father. 'We've got loads of labels, most of which we can read, but we don't know a great deal about many of them. When I've tried to look them up on the internet, often they aren't there. And some of the others seem to have changed their names.'

'Oh yes,' laughed Steve. 'Some of those old plants have half a dozen or more synonyms.'

'Synonyms?' asked Elsie.

'Different words for the same thing,' explained Steve. 'In the old days if an eminent botanist said he'd got a new plant and named it, after a bit of research it was usually accepted.'

'It's not actually that straightforward, is it Dad?' prompted Ken.

'Oh no!' groaned Stella.

'Ken and I were looking up one particular plant that Ellen Willmott grew,' explained Steve. 'It was called *Lilium thomsonianum*. We looked it up and there were two synonyms given. One said it was a synonym of *Notholirion thomsonianum*; the other said it was a synonym of *Notholirion bulbiferum*. When we looked both those up, they were both accepted names, i.e. two different plants, named by two different botanists.'

'Which name did you choose?' asked Elsie.

'Neither,' said Steve. 'We decided that if they couldn't work it out, then we'd just stick with the original name.'

'Which just goes to show,' said Ken, 'that there is absolutely no need to feel embarrassed about being confused about plant names, when even the experts can't always agree.'

'Are you still enjoying Warley Place?' asked Stella, looking at Elsie.

'Oh yes, and the more I learn, the more I enjoy it,' replied Elsie.

'And you are still doing your lovely sketches?'

'I've done a few, yes.'

'Not a few, there must be approaching one hundred now,' said Ken. 'I'm keeping them in a special folder.'

'They're not good enough for that,' blushed Elsie. 'And anyway, photographs are much better.'

'No, I think many would disagree with that,' said Steve. 'A good watercolour can pick out all the important features useful for identification, and can also look beautiful. Just look at Ellen Willmott's book 'The Genus Rosa' – or, better still, see Alfred Parsons' originals in the RHS Lindley Library.'

'Your pictures are, from what I've seen, good enough to be bound and even perhaps published one day,' said

Stella. 'Though I don't suppose you'll have much time once baby comes. Try to get at least one day off. We'll look after it, or perhaps your mum could. Then you can relax and do sketching, or go to Warley Place, or just do nothing.'

'Has everyone finished?' asked Stella. 'Oh yes, and the final etiquette lesson, Elsie – and Ken and Steve. In a restaurant, when you have finished, put the knife and fork diagonally across the plate. I've never done it myself, but perhaps at a very posh restaurant you might wonder why others are doing it and you can follow suit. And you certainly don't try to be helpful and stack the empty plates for them. It might seem like good manners, and actually I think it's a nice way of saying thank-you, but it's not according to good etiquette. Now, ice cream?'

'Oh yes, please,' said Elsie.

'One final thing about etiquette,' said Stella. 'You mustn't click your fingers to get the waiter's attention to tell him you'd like the dessert. You just say "Fetch the ice cream, will you Steve, dear?" It usually works.'

Rolling his eyes, Steve got up and, accompanied by Ken, went to the kitchen to fetch the dessert.

'Thank you so much for your help, Stella,' said Elsie. 'I'd hate to let Ken down at one of those dinners he goes to.'

'I must admit I had a few misgivings at first,' Stella replied. 'But not for long. You are very good for him, a wife – and a daughter-in-law – to be proud of. Strange, isn't it, how suddenly something can happen that changes the direction your life is taking. Or, in Ken's case, wasn't taking. He was just drifting along, with no great interest in anything.'

'Well it's nothing compared with the change it's made to my life,' said Elsie.

'There's one question I'd like to ask about etiquette,' said Ken as he and Steve came in with the ice cream and dessert bowls.

'Yes dear?' said his mother.

'It's about the size of the tip for the waiter, and whether you are going to leave it discretely on the table or let us have it later.'

'The size of the tip depends on the service provided,' said Stella. 'But we'll make an exception in your case and you can have the full ten percent. You're good at maths Steve, what's ten percent of ....'

'Yes, yes, I know, nothing,' said Steve. 'You should be ashamed, getting out of it on a technicality.'

'Do you feel ashamed, Elsie?' asked Stella.

'No, I don't,' laughed Elsie.

17

Edward talks to Jacob
August 1934

'That was an excellent meal, thank you very much Mrs Maurer,' said Edward patting his stomach.

'Maggie, please,' she said.

'Thank you, and I'm Edward of course.'

'Will you stay for a glass of dandelion wine?' asked Jacob. 'Oh, but I forgot, you are a Quaker.'

'Quakers aren't necessarily teetotal,' explained Edward. 'But those of us that do drink do so in moderation, so a glass of your wine would be very acceptable. But I don't want to intrude on your evening.'

'Not at all,' said Maggie. 'We usually just chat while we listen to the radio, but I think the battery is nearly flat now and needs to be recharged, so you'll be doing us a favour.'

'You've both been at Warley Place for some time I believe,' commented Edward.

'Oh yes,' replied Jacob. 'She asked my employer if he could spare me when I was a young nineteen year old boy. I was very flattered so, as I think I've told you, I came over from Switzerland about forty years ago.'

'Do you regret it?'

'Oh dear no. I haven't made much money but I've been very happy, especially when Maggie and I got together. I am a very lucky man.'

'It's hard work though, isn't it?'

'Oh yes,' said Jacob, rubbing his knees. 'There is so much kneeling and bending, and in the cold wet weather it takes its toll on one's joints.'

'So how did you meet Maggie?'

'We met at the bothy where Jacob lodged before he was married,' said Maggie. 'It was run by my father and mother for all Miss Willmott's unmarried staff. I must confess I was a little envious when Jacob went back home to get married to Rosina, but I understood.'

'Then when Rosina died,' Jacob broke in, 'Maggie became mother to my nine children and they all loved her as much as I did.'

'Your niece Friedi helped look after them for a few years before we got together again,' Maggie reminded him.

'That's true,' acknowledged Jacob, 'but it was you they really loved. It was good of Friedi to come, but she was a bit strict!'

What about you?' asked Maggie. 'Do you have children?'

'Yes, I do,' said Edward. 'Jacob has presumably told you my dear wife Margaret died some time ago and my only son Howard has joined the Royal Air Force. He is a pilot. He thinks this chap Hitler is stirring things up and there could be another war if we don't arm ourselves and make them realise they can't win another conflict.'

'Is your son not a Quaker then?'

'Yes, but he feels that what he is doing will prevent a war. I respect his decision. He might even be right. I'm not sure I could do it, but rationalising it I realise that my continuing peaceful existence might depend on people like him.'

Jacob placed a glass of golden wine in front of him.

'Tell me truly what you think of it,' he asked anxiously. Edward took a sip.

'My goodness, if anything was going entice me away from my moderate ways that would be it,' he said.

'I've been very lucky working here,' said Jacob sipping his own glass. 'I've learned so much. I doubt if there is another alpine garden in Europe to match this one. Goodness knows what will happen to it when Miss Willmott dies though, it needs so much attention.'

'Would the Royal Horticultural Society take it on?' asked Maggie.

'I doubt it,' said Jacob. 'It would take a lot of time and money keeping this place going. I expect it will pass to the Berkeley family but they have enough to do looking after their own estate in Worcester. I expect they'll sell it, but I can't imagine who would want to buy it.'

'Whatever happens,' said Edward, putting his now empty glass down, 'you will be remembered for your work here.' He looked puzzled. 'I don't know how I know that, but I do.'

'I think that's the wine talking,' suggested Jacob. 'It's just wishful thinking. Would you try the Blackberry? It's very good.'

'Just a small one.'

'It's not as if I have any flowers named after me.'

'Oh yes, Miss Willmott has many named after her I believe. But one day you will have one too. I know that.'

'I don't think so,' said Jacob, sipping at his own glass.

'It would be nice though,' said Maggie. 'You deserve it as much as she does.'

'No, if I had decided not to come here someone else would have done my work. But if Miss Willmott hadn't

173

had the idea in the first place and poured time and money into it there would have been no alpine garden. She deserves her fame.'

'Your part will be recognised,' insisted Edward.

'It's getting dark,' said Jacob rising to light the Aladdin oil lamp on the table.

'And it's time I was going,' said Edward, rising also. 'Come on Rufus.'

Somewhat reluctantly Rufus raised his head and eased himself up from the floor.

'Sorry about the dog hairs,' Edward apologised.

'We've had a lot worse,' laughed Maggie, 'and they are soon removed.'

'And thank you for the food and the wine, both were magnificent,' continued Edward.

'Thank you for your company,' said Jacob. 'I have enjoyed the evening.'

It was a warm night and he glanced at the tables outside the Thatchers pub only a few yards from Jacob's cottage. Rufus gave a low growl as they passed by and Edward noticed someone turning his head away as they drew near. The light was poor, but he seemed familiar, with a black and red kerchief, very like the ruffian who had looked as if he was going to rob Ellen Willmott on the way from the station those few weeks ago. The other one, Edward was sure, was the fellow Nigel who had wanted to work at Warley Place. There was nothing to be gained by approaching them, so he walked on.

* * *

Bertie's companion, Nigel, stretched his mouth in a humourless grin.

'You don't like him, do you?'

'Nah. Trouble is, he's always got that bloody great dog with him.'

'What's he done to you?'

'Just stopped me getting me hands on a nice fat purse, Nige, that's what 'e did.'

'Oh, the Willmott woman's, yes, you told me about that. I didn't know he was the bloke who stopped you.'

'Yeah. I'd still like to get my hands on some of 'er money though. Rolling in it, she must be. Not fair, rich people like 'er 'aving all that, us workers with nothing.'

'I think tonight might be the time to do something about it.'

'What? I thought she sussed you out?'

'No, it was just that the other bloke, Saxon I think she called him, complicated things a bit. Got a bit too risky.'

'So, she did suss you out.'

'No, and drop it, right? We're going ahead.'

'But we don't know where the stuff is.'

'I've had a word. The windows on the conservatory are mostly rotten enough they can be removed without making a noise. Then just along a bit in the house is her chapel.'

'So we go in there and pray she doesn't come down and catch us?'

'Don't try to be funny. There's gold stuff in there. Crosses and things. That'll teach her to - '

'So she did turn you down then?'

'I told you, shut it. I almost hope she does come and catch us ...'

He pulled a big long bayonet from inside his jacket and rubbed his finger up and down the edge.

'... then we can work in peace.'

'No, not that,' said an alarmed Bertie. 'I don't do stabbing people. It ain't right. You get strung up for that.'

'Only if you are caught.'

'Doesn't the butler chap stay there?' asked Bertie.

'Sometimes. I saw him go past earlier though, so not tonight. You in on it?'

'No fear. I've heard she 'as a gun.'

Nigel frowned. 'Then I'll just have to make sure she doesn't get a chance to use it.'

'One of my old man's mates went there one night and never came back,' said Bertie. 'Wally, 'is name was. Just leave it alone. Or do it another night when you've got a little less beer in you.'

'No,' said Nigel wiping his lips on a handkerchief. 'I told you, she's not getting away with it. It's dark now and there's gold in there waiting for us.'

'What if that gardener in the lodge sees you going past?'

'He won't. There's a small gate along the road so we won't have to go past his place. There's lots of cover between there and the house. I know what I'm doing.'

'Well let's 'ope she don't know what you are doing too,' said Bertie. 'I'm off. See you tomorrow. If you are still around.'

'Your turning your back on all that gold? Scared to break into a house because there's an old woman there? She's upstairs and fast asleep, probably deaf as a post.'

'Well, OK, but no violence.'

Nigel sat there thinking, waiting for it to get darker. It was true, there was a rumour that she carried a pistol and no doubt there were shotguns in the house. But they'd be very careful and if there wasn't an easy window or door, they could always come back another time. She was rich. He wasn't. She probably wouldn't even miss it. And if she did catch them, well, there was always....

He thought of his old wartime bayonet inside his coat. It was very sharp; he had made sure before they left. It was his father's. He'd found it when the old man died. They said it was his liver; too much drinking. But after what he went through in the war what did they expect? He'd jump out of his skin every time anyone dropped something and when a car backfired once he couldn't stop shaking for over an hour. What did he get for it? A miserable pension and no job. He did his best to make sure Nigel did better though, taught him how to con the rich ones – it served them right, if they wouldn't give people jobs.

Eventually, as everyone left the pub, they made their slightly unsteady way down the road towards Brentwood. Two men suffering the effects of drink wouldn't attract any attention at that time of night, but later they would look very suspicious. They would get in the grounds, wait in the trees for a while. He'd brought a couple of bottles, so they could drink for a bit then do the job when it was really dark.

What concerned Nigel most was that people said she was actually broke and he wouldn't find any money. There would certainly be stuff in the chapel, and jewellery somewhere, surely, bound to have some diamonds there. They'd be in a safe no doubt though, and he couldn't do safes. Unless there was a key somewhere. Bound to be something he could sell. Everyone knew she had some nice musical stuff there, so he could pinch a fiddle or something and flog that. No, the religious stuff was probably the best, it would melt down nicely.

The gate appeared and they stopped, looking about. No cars, no-one walking, totally silent now. It squeaked a bit as he opened it, and they crept in.

It was a pitch black moonless night already, and Nigel swore as he stumbled over a rock, annoyed that Bertie was following on behind letting him find all the obstacles.

The path was overgrown, hardly a path any more, but led to a wider track which meandered its way through some rockeries, but he choked back an obscenity and ducked down as a rose climbing an arbour sawed his face with its thorns. Trying to go round the rose he edged into the narrow path of a rockery.

He stopped to catch his breath and sat on something hard and sharp. It was one of her plant labels and he yanked it out and threw it into the darkness.

'Right,' he whispered. 'We wait for half an hour, then do it. She's bound to be asleep by then, all oldies are.'

They sat on the side of the rockery and he pulled the bottles out of his pocket, passing one to Bertie.

'Cor, look at that,' whispered Bertie, looking up at the long strip of densely packed stars stretching across the black sky.

'That's the Milky Way, that is,' said Nigel.

They looked up at it, spellbound by its beauty.

They sat looking at it for a few minutes, then Nigel looked towards where he thought the house was, but he was no longer sure.

'There's no lights on,' he said. 'Might as well get it over with.'

But he realised he'd lost his sense of direction. He just didn't know quite where he was. It was as if the eerie blackness had wrapped itself round them. He became aware of something. A sound? Just the rustling of the trees, almost as if they were talking to him; or about him. He got up and tried to move but his foot was caught in brambles that dug into his ankles and he fell full length between two rocks. Cursing, he pulled his knife out and started slashing but a particularly vicious stinging nettle sprung up and wiped his face while a bramble dug its thorns into his wrist.

178

'God, I hate that woman,' he spat through clenched teeth. 'Why's she let her bloody garden get like this? I'll teach her a lesson she won't forget.' He pulled his bayonet out and started slashing with it.

He had no idea how far the impenetrable growth stretched, but eventually they got to the main drive.

'We'll go along a bit and see whether there's any lights on,' he whispered. 'Couldn't see properly from where we were.'

They edged their way along until they were at the top of the ha-ha wall, then walked to get a better view of the house. It was still very dark.

'Watch it Nige, there's a big drop down there into the ditch,' said Bertie very quietly.

'What did you say?' said Nigel, turning his head to hear better.

'Watch the drop on your left.'

'OK,' he replied, turning his head back just in time to smack it into the trunk of a tree.

He froze, fuming with rage. His legs hurt, his hands hurt, and now his face hurt – but his pride hurt most of all. He pulled his bayonet out again.

'I'm going to get her,' he snarled. 'I'll make her sorry.'

'Wait Nigel,' pleaded Bertie. 'We just wanted the money, remember? That'll hurt 'er most of all. Put that bloody knife away.'

They stood in silence, looking at the house.

'Was that voices?' asked Bertie anxiously.

'No,' said Nigel, not sounding very convinced. The murmuring did actually sound like voices, some distance away.

The branches of the trees seemed to swish as if they were talking to each other. He didn't think there was enough wind about for that.

'Calm down,' he told himself. 'Revenge is best served cold.'

He slid his bayonet out again and ran his fingers along the edge.

He realised there was a strange very faint rattling noise, like a hand cart, coming from up by the coach house, and the voices were louder.

'I don't like this,' whispered Bertie.

'Just relax,' said a very nervous Nigel. 'It's just your imagination.'

The trees were noisier now, the strange noise was getting closer.

A bat suddenly flew in front of his face; he gasped and jumped back.

Bertie heard the crack as Nigel disappeared over the edge of the ha-ha, into the ditch.

'Are you OK Nige?'

The sound of the cart had faded away and the trees were silent.

'Nige?'

Bertie made his way to the end of the wall, climbed down and then stumbled along until he found Nigel. The moon had come out and shed enough light to see the rock upon which Nigel had hit his head. The bayonet was sticking out of his body. There was no sound of breathing, and his head was at a very unnatural angle.

'Oh Gawd,' said Bertie to himself. 'E's broke 'is bloody neck.'

Lots of people had seen him with Nigel earlier, and probably also saw them walking up the road together. They would never believe he hadn't done it. He crouched there for a few minutes, waiting to see if anyone had heard and hoping that Nigel would wake up, but knowing his neck was well and truly broken. They'd definitely not believe him. He'd have to hide the body. He made an attempt to pick it up, but he already knew Nigel was too heavy. He'd got a few hours yet, before the earliest workers came in, but what could he do? Get it away from the front of the house, that's for sure.

He got hold of the arms, and managed to drag Nigel along the ditch towards the rockeries. Parts were so overgrown there was a chance he wouldn't be found for a while, then he'd be seen as a burglar who'd come unstuck and no-one would think Bertie had anything to do with it. Except they'd see someone had hidden the body, he realised. Even so, there was no alternative. He'd ask people if they'd seen Nigel lately, and look concerned.

He was just about all in when he neared the end of the ditch and the edge of the first rockery. Gritting his teeth, he pushed the brambles aside with his back as he dragged the body into them, just before the ground rose again. Grimacing, he pulled the bayonet out and started to dig with that and his hands. It was an hour or more before he was satisfied that the hole was deep enough and he dragged the body into it. Then he got enough earth, leaves and general garden detritus to cover the body.

She's never going to work in this part of the garden again, he persuaded himself. No-one is going to dig here. Why should they? He threw the bayonet away – being caught with that would be a dead give-away – and, crouching down, made his slow and painful way to the gate. His legs hurt, his arms hurt, his face hurt – everything hurt. Damn the bloody woman. He'd miss Nigel, with his funny ways. He was pretty useless at everything except conning people, but good company.

18

Tea Break
September 2013

'We've just got enough mortar left for one more brick, then it's tea break I think,' said Donald as he carefully ran his trowel along his already neat pointing. It was only a low wall, by the cold frames, but still needed to look right.

'Could you pass me the level?' he asked.

Robert stepped back and slipped, almost falling.

'Oops, sorry, I've stepped in the mortar,' he apologised.

'Don't worry,' said Donald, 'scrape it off your boots, it's a shame to waste it.'

An embarrassed Robert did just that and moved the board on which the last of the mortar mix lay next to Donald, who deftly scooped it up and flopped it onto the bottom and end of a brick and slapped it in place. A quick wipe with his trowel and it was finished apart from needing a brush after tea.

Taking their gloves and knee pads off they made their way to the conservatory, which was where volunteers had their tea break when weather permitted. Today was perfect – dry and sunny but not too hot.

The others were all there, but space was found for Donald and Robert and they delved into their rucksacks for drinks and food.

'Bit late Robert, is Donald overworking you?' said Gordon, taking a sip from his flask of coffee.

'No,' said Robert ruefully. 'I accidentally stepped in the mix just as Donald was about to use it for the last brick.'

'My goodness,' said Gordon. 'I bet you were mortarfied!'

Robert groaned and Gordon ducked as Robert threw a glove at him, then threw it back.

'I've had an idea for our next spring public days,' said Harry, who was always looking for ways to make money for the Trust and for Warley Place in particular. 'We can plant some daffodil bulbs and sell them to visitors.'

'What, dig up bulbs from here?' said Daphne, frowning. 'I'm not sure we should do that.'

'No, buy them in bulk commercially but grow them on here. Ken can get them for us. We can make it clear that that's what we've done. I know someone who will pot them for us, then let us have them to look after until spring. I think they'll all sell, but if they don't they can be sold at Thorndon.'

'Sounds like a good idea,' said Beverley.

'The squirrels will dig them up,' said Norman.

'We'll put chicken wire over the top,' said Harry.

'Then the shoots will grow through the chicken wire and we won't be able to get it off.'

'We'll remove the chicken wire before that happens,' said Harry patiently. 'We can erect a chicken wire fence which will stop rabbits and deter squirrels. They'll find something easier.'

'Perhaps we could advertise it in advance,' suggested Peter. 'A piece in the website perhaps?'

'I could do that,' said Gordon. 'I could include a short poem, too.'

'Oh no!' groaned Harry.

'What is this world if full of tea, we have no time to stand and -'

'Gordon!' said Daphne.

Looking very hurt, Gordon continued, 'see, the daffodils as they grow tall.'

'I don't think Wordsworth would think much of that,' said Beryl, who used to be a teacher.

'Composed by Wordsmirth,' explained Gordon. 'Wordsworth pinched the idea from him.' He sighed. 'But since no-one else shares my appreciation of poetry I'll leave it out and let you see it, Harry, before I post it.'

'By the way,' said Donald, 'Where is Ken? Not like him to miss a Monday.'

'Elsie's pretty near her time,' said Anne. 'I don't suppose he'd want to leave her in case they had to dash to the hospital.'

'I've just had a bright idea,' said Harry.

They all looked at him while he ignored comments like 'That's a first' and 'Don't worry it will soon pass'.

'Since we've finished our tea and there's still an hour and a half until lunch time, why don't we get on with some work.'

'I suppose it will pass the time well enough' agreed Gordon, as they all got to their feet with a certain amount of groaning and rubbing of knees.

'Daphne, Bev, Anne, you OK to continue with the bonfire?' asked Harry.

'I was going to bag up some leaf mould if someone could help,' said Anne.

Peter volunteered so they walked off to the container in the ha-ha ditch by the walnut tree.

'We should be able to finish the wall with one more mix,' said Donald, and he and Robert made their way back to the cold frame area.

Others carried on with their various tasks – clearing leaves, pruning back shrubs intruding on to the paths, pulling sycamore seedlings etc. and, satisfied that all were usefully occupied, Harry went for a tour round the various workplaces to make sure that all was well.

Robert looked up from his bricks at the sound of footsteps as Harry approached and saw someone else hurriedly trying to catch up. It was Ken, grinning from ear to ear, and they arrived at the wall at the same time.

'It's a girl,' he said. 'Both doing well. They are sleeping at the moment and mum and dad are with them so I thought I'd come and tell you rather than phone.'

'Congratulations,' they all said, stripping gloves off and shaking his hand.

'Have you got a name yet?' asked Donald.

'Yes, I'm Ken, like I've always been. But not for the baby, no.'

'That's tricky. Both mothers would like her named after them but if so which would be the first name? As we said before, we quite liked Laura, but wondered about Ellen. After all, if it wasn't for Ellen Willmott, Elsie and I would never have met and we wouldn't have had any children together.'

'Well good luck with that. Of course, you could have more than two forenames. What are the names of the grandmothers?'

'Stella and Mary.'

'OK, Laura Mary Stella Bradshaw. Oh dear, sounds a bit steam trainish?'

They stared blankly.

'The initials, LMS, London Midland and Scottish railways. A bit before your time Ken. And Bradshaw's was a railway timetable, wasn't it?'

He thought for a moment.

'How about a nice horticultural set of initials? Ellen Laura Mary Stella – ELMS.'

'I think we'd better leave it to them,' suggested Harry.

'Go on Ken, go round and tell the others, they'll all be delighted. And make sure you bring the baby as soon as she can travel.'

'That must be the first time a volunteer has given birth, mustn't it?' suggested Harry. 'While they are working here,' added quickly as Robert opened his mouth. 'Or rather, during the time they were volunteers at Warley Place.'

'Probably,' said Robert. 'In the same month as Ellen Willmott died. As Ken said, without Ellen Willmott and Warley Place this particular baby would never have existed. Pity Ellen Willmott didn't know that, it might have made her feel better about not having children of her own.'

'I feel sorry for Jacob Maurer, too,' said Donald. 'He saw the garden he'd cared for all his working life go to rack and ruin before he died, and nothing to remember him by. If only he'd known about his daffodil.'

Some years before, the volunteers had asked the famous daffodil breeder Ron Scamp if he had a daffodil waiting for a name. He sent some pictures and the Research Group chose one, which was registered as *Narcissus* 'Jacob Maurer'. A few had been planted in front of his old cottage, some in volunteers' gardens and some over Rosina Maurer's burial place.

'I think that's finished now,' said Robert, as he smoothed the last bit of pointing between the final two bricks. 'I expect the leaf mould packers could do with some help while we wait for it to dry.'

Once the trowel, the spade and the board had been washed they walked over to the leaf mould pit at the end of the ha-ha, where the trailer was standing. Peter and Anne were just climbing out, a row of bags full of leaf mould lining the bottom of the wall.

'Just in time,' said a relieved-looking Peter.

Donald and Robert dropped down into the pit and heaved up the bags, while Peter and Anne loaded them on to the trailer, about thirty in all.

Donald volunteered to drive. Well, driving was a bit of a euphemism. The contraption towing the trailer was an old rotavator, converted by David. It was steered by wide handlebars at the front, and the operator started the engine by pulling a cord and then adjusting a small lever on the handlebars to alter the speed of the engine, and another one, like the brake on a bicycle, to operate the clutch. Once it was going, he walked alongside, while, because the contraption had no brakes, the others got ready for the down-hill section of the drive.

To their surprise it spluttered into life at first pull of the cord, and they were soon making ribald comments about Donald's driving ability as it put-putted its way down the carriage drive, bouncing and weaving on the uneven surface. Although it did sound a little like a tractor, it wasn't particularly noisy and they were able to chat between themselves (volunteers do tend to talk a lot, everywhere) until they reached the car park. Once there they unloaded the bags and Peter took the helm to steer them back up the hill.

'Thank goodness David made this machine up,' commented Robert. 'Remember when we had to pull it? At our age, it's surprising no-one had a heart attack.'

'I know a couple who always made themselves scarce when the cart needed to be pulled anywhere,' laughed Donald. 'And who can blame them?'

'I wonder what Ellen Willmott's gardeners did,' said Robert. 'Presumably used wheelbarrows.'

'I used one to take a load up here on a wheelbarrow

once,' said Peter. 'I didn't like it. The old heart was pumping away when I got to the top.'

'Funny, though,' said Robert, looking into the trees lining the path. 'I often get the feeling we're being watched.'

'That's because you spend so much time looking through those dusty old archives,' said Peter. 'Found anything interesting lately?'

'Well they're all interesting. The biggest problem is reading the handwritten letters from those days. Oh, that and finding out when they were written, they rarely seem to put the year in, even if there's a date at all. Sometimes it's just 'Tuesday', or 'Tuesday 1st'.'

'But you can get a picture of what she was like?'

'Oh yes,' said Robert. 'I know you were joking, but I can really imagine her being here.'

'Do you think you would have liked her?' asked Donald, opening the throttle a bit to get up the slope.

Robert thought for a moment.

'I don't think I would have done,' he said. 'Not from the way she treated Jacob. But she did a number of very generous and warm-hearted things that I wouldn't have known about then. So perhaps the true answer, if I had known what I know now, is that sometimes I would have liked her, and sometimes not.'

'But didn't she fritter away all her money?'

'No, she provided work for a lot of people. Yes, she did travel about a lot, but she did so mostly using coach and horses locally, and trains and ships for long journeys. So she didn't contribute to climate change in the way that people do today. Yes, she bought a couple of mansions in Europe, but the First World War was at least partly responsible for that poor investment.'

'Do you think she really is watching us?'

'I wouldn't be surprised!' laughed Robert.

'Strange she didn't get married.'

'Yes, she was beautiful early on in her life, and looked it in the photographs too. Perhaps suitors were put off by the speed at which she spent her money and preferred not to be broke!'

'Damn!' said Robert, looking through the rhododendrons. 'There's a dog. A great big one. I'm sure it was, just behind the *Trochodendron*.'

'You sure? I can't see it,' said Peter. 'Maybe a deer?'

'No, not a deer. Oh well, it's not there now. Must have imagined it.'

They reached the top.

'No more to take down,' said Anne. 'Not today, anyway. Next Monday will do.'

Donald and Peter put the machines away, while Robert went to brush down the pointing on his wall.

'That's it for today,' said Harry. 'There's no point in starting anything else, so let's go home. Thanks everybody.'

They grabbed their bags and wandered back down the drive, chatting noisily.

Peter noticed Robert looking at the *Trochodendron*, a puzzled frown on his face.

19

September 1934
Peace at Last

Edward tried the window ventilator in the greenhouse. As he had promised when he first came to Warley Place, he had cannibalised two of the hothouses to make the other two fully functional. It hadn't been easy, but with a lot of filing, oiling and painting he was pleased with the result.

'What do you think, Rufus?' he asked.

His dog, laying alongside on the path, did not bother to raise its head nor to answer his question, but did deign to roll its eyes up to look at him.

'Miss Willmott's looking very tired today, don't you think?'

Rufus lifted his head at the sound of her name.

'She really ought to be taking it easy at her time of life,' he continued.

'And what time of life is that pray?' came a rather shrill voice, at the sound of which Rufus got to his feet with his tail wagging.

She delved into her pocket and slipped a tasty morsel to a grateful Rufus and ruffled his head, then sat on the stub wall of the adjacent ruined greenhouse.

'You know very well you are doing too much,' said Edward, neither surprised nor disconcerted by her sudden appearance. 'You are looking particularly tired today.'

He started packing the tools into his wheelbarrow.

'You are making me uncomfortable standing,' she said. 'Have you a moment?'

'Certainly.' He sat on a pile of bricks, slightly uncomfortable but not too much so.

'I really would like to thank you for what you have done here,' she offered.

'Is there a 'but' coming?' he asked. 'Would you like me to go?'

'No, not at all. But I have learned rather late in the day that one should thank those who help them before it's too late. If it's you who is left there is only remorse. If it is the other who is left, he will wonder if he was appreciated,' she said. 'Or loved.'

'An excellent philosophy,' commented Edward. 'But there is no need for thanks. I have gained far more than I have given. Jacob and Robinson are the ones who have given all those years of loyal service and still do. I know they are your employees, but thanking them would do so much for them – and, I feel, for you.'

She nodded, thoughtfully.

'You have a point,' she said. 'I will think on it.'

They sat in silence for a while.

'How quiet it is,' she said. 'I suppose you are used to that; sitting in silence.'

'I am. Charles Lamb once wrote, in one of his essays, *'What a balm and a solace it is, to go and seat yourself, for a quiet half hour, upon some undisputed corner of a bench, among the gentle Quakers!'* But I have to confess that sitting here amongst the flowers and the trees is in some ways even more peaceful than sitting inside four walls and a roof.'

'The trees almost talk to one, don't they?' she whispered, then sang quietly.

> *'Far from the noisy throng, by song birds lulled to rest;*
> *Where rock the branches high by breezes soft caressed.'*

'That's very poetic,' said Edward. 'Where does it come from?'

From an opera,' she said wistfully. 'Jocelyn' by Benjamin Godard. It's a lullaby. I sing it sometimes to the child I never had.'

'One of those ripples just never came your way then,' said Edward.

'Alas no. Some came close by, but not close enough.'

In an obvious attempt to change the subject, she asked:

'In your Quaker Meeting for Worship,' she said. 'How do you worship when you have no proper service, no altar, nothing on which to demonstrate how you feel?'

'Calling it 'worship' is perhaps a bit misleading. We don't sit there reassuring God that he or she is doing a jolly good job. We try to understand what is required of us to make the world a better place. Some Friends may rise and speak about what they are feeling and others may continue the theme.'

'It must be difficult speaking in that way in front of others, in case you do not make your feelings clear and misunderstandings arise.'

'Yes, that can be so. But remember that for those who believe God is listening, it should perhaps be even more daunting to speak in front of Him.'

'I suppose so. But I do not think God would misunderstand. But you have said previously that you are uncertain about whether or not there is a God.'

'That is true. When a ship sinks the survivors may give thanks to God for saving them; but the relatives of those who never came home do not accuse God of letting their kinfolk die.'

'That is no reason for there not being a God,' she pointed out.

'You are correct. But it does question whether, even if there is a God, there is any point in worshipping Him.'

'What about music? You do not sing hymns, do you?'

'No. I love music, but hymns are a problem. It's the words, you see.'

'What's wrong with the words? They are often so uplifting.'

'That's true. But if you sing 'All things bright and beautiful, the Lord God made them all' perhaps you should add that he also made things that are not so beautiful, like plagues, famines, earthquakes, cannibalistic insects and the like.'

'So do you believe in a life after death?' she asked.

Edward pondered this question, as he had done so often in the past.

'Truthfully, I know not,' he said. 'If there is, it will be very different from the one we are experiencing at the moment.'

He looked at her shadow, stretched across the bricks.

'If you were a two-dimensional being, like that shadow,' he said, 'you could not possibly understand what it was like being a three dimensional being, as we are. Similarly, I do not think we could ever really imagine what the next step, analogous to a fourth dimension, would be like. But anyway, as I said some time ago, the ripples will continue long after we have gone, and yours will be big ripples indeed. Your life will continue for many a year.'

She sat deep in thought. Eventually Edward spoke again.

'I have a meeting to go to this evening,' he said. 'I would like to leave now if I may. But please think about Jacob and Robinson.'

'Thank you for your honesty and for your advice,' she said. 'And have a fine evening.'

He left her there, a lonely figure sitting on the ruins of one of her greenhouses. Rufus seemed uncertain about following Edward, but with a backward glance and a whimper, did so and hurried (as much as he ever did hurry) to catch up.

* * *

'Gertrude Jekyll may have been right,' said Jacob Maurer to James Robinson as they stood by the conservatory at the rear of the big house. 'Ellen Willmott probably was the greatest woman gardener of her day. In fact as far as I am concerned she still is. But that doesn't mean she hasn't got eccentric and rather crabby in her old age. And as for the way she treats people, it's nineteen thirty-four for goodness' sake, the world's a different place now. She's still living in the nineteenth century.'

Jacob fiddled with his huge moustache. It made his already sad looking face even sadder but he wouldn't shave it off. Small in stature and quiet in nature he preferred the time when James Preece was in charge, leaving him to concentrate on his alpine garden. He had neither the appearance of a head gardener nor, if the truth were known, the inclination, and did in fact prefer to work alone. The reverse was not the case however, the few staff left on the estate all vying for the chance to work with Jacob Maurer; there were none to equal him as far as alpine plants were concerned and he was always happy to pass on his hard won knowledge.

Looking after all these grounds was impossible and would have been so however good a manager he was, for he no longer had the staff to manage. The numbers had dwindled from a peak of about a hundred at one time to a mere handful now. Even the forty-five acres remaining of the original Warley Place estate was far too much for those few that were left, and it was rapidly deteriorating into a jungle while they concentrated on a few select areas.

'It's all right for you,' said James Robinson. 'You're still young, not yet turned sixty, and you can lose yourself in your alpine garden. I'm seventy-three and at her beck and call all the time while she's in the house, which has been more and more lately. Where is she anyway?'

Robinson was a tall and distinguished person, easy to talk to and with the ability to calm things down when trouble loomed – which was a big asset in the current times. As her various so-called friends had deserted her at approximately the same rate as her fortunes dwindled he had become her close confidant rather than the butler he once was.

'Looking round the rockery I think. She hasn't been walking round much at all these last couple of weeks. She's not doing badly at all though for a rheumatic seventy-six year old. Actually I miss her not creeping up on me to see what I'm up to. It used to drive the men mad but I liked having someone who was interested in what I was doing and knowledgeable enough to argue with me about how to do it.'

'I suppose you wouldn't still be here if you didn't like her. How long is it now?'

'Forty years. It's been good, most of it. Where else would I have got the opportunity to build an alpine garden like hers?'

'I've been butler here for forty-four years. Eighteen-ninety I started. And yes, she's done well. I can moan about her to you, Jacob, because I know you feel the same as I do. For all her eccentricity and sharp remarks, she's a lovely person. She doesn't ask anyone to put up with what she wouldn't put up with herself.'

He waved his hand at the big house.

'Look at that, for instance. Library, Music Room, Chapel, Dining Room, Morning Room, sixteen bedrooms, God knows how many other rooms, and what does she do? She lives in one room with an oil stove! Her own dining room, and she has bread and cheese for lunch!'

They were silent for a while, watching a robin scratching in the earth.

'What does she want us for anyway?' asked Jacob.

'I don't know. It's a bit unusual, I must say. You're gardens, I'm house. Neither of us can cope, that's about the only thing we have in common.'

'And that we are her two most loyal servants,' suggested Jacob.

'Loyal or not, we can't live on fresh air.'

'But at least if anything happens to her you'll still have a roof over your head,' said Jacob. 'I'll be thrown out of South Lodge with nowhere to go and if her finances are as bad as they seem to be then I'll have no pension either.'

'How on earth did it come to this?' asked Robinson. 'She built Warley Place up to something wonderful, now it's worse than when the Willmott family moved in. It might have been different had she married but who would have put up with her?'

They were quiet again for a bit. The robin had departed for a more fruitful area so they contented themselves with watching for Ellen Willmott's appearance at the conservatory door to usher them in.

'September is nearly over,' said Jacob, 'and so is summer. I like autumn though. I like spring better, but autumn is fine.'

Robinson consulted his pocket watch. 'It's six o'clock.'

'Oh dear, there's some balsam in the border,' said Jacob, fidgeting. 'I must at least clear it from the sight of the house even if it is rife elsewhere.'

'Things are difficult at the moment,' said Robinson.

Jacob took a few steps and pulled several of the yellow flowered weeds from the ground, stuffed them in his pocket and walked back to join his colleague.

'Whatever it's like for us, it must be ten times worse for her,' he said eventually. 'She's a wonderful person who has great talent and had plans to match. Extravagant, yes, but the war must have played havoc with her investments. There will never be another like her.'

'You are right there,' agreed Robinson. 'A wonderful person.'

'Not so wonderful,' said a high pitched voice behind them.

True to form, she had come back the long way round through the coach house and the walled garden, approaching them from the rear. They both knew that, suspicious as always, she wanted to hear what they were saying about her. After all these years of loyal service she still couldn't accept that these two people loved and respected her as they did.

Although not a pretty woman in the traditional feminine sense, she was striking in appearance. Even with her small, though by no means diminutive, stature, she radiated authority by means of her piercing eyes and regal carriage, her advanced age notwithstanding. She had long since given up dressing to suit her position, but somehow the casual though sombre clothes advertised the fact that she did not need to enhance her natural authority by covering herself in fine linen.

'Come on in,' she said, opening the conservatory door and walking through. 'I'm hungry. Cheese and some of that nice bread James? No, Jacob, no need to remove your boots, this floor has seen far worse.'

Jacob smiled to himself. If he had left them on she would have told him to remove them.

'My feet are aching,' he said. 'I have brought some shoes if you don't mind.'

By the time he had changed into more comfortable footwear Robinson had reappeared with a tray on which were heaped bread, butter, cheese, plates and knives; a jug of water and some glasses were already on the table. He unloaded the tray, put it aside and the three of them settled into their chairs.

'The estate is in a mess, isn't it,' she said as she buttered a thick slice of bread and cut some cheese. 'That is not a criticism of either of you, no-one could do more. It is just a statement of fact. What do you think?'

She would have given a sharp retort to any attempt at a denial, but neither of the two men wanted openly to agree with her, however true her statement might be.

'Well?'

'Things are difficult, it's true,' said Jacob eventually. 'The outer parts of the garden are indeed not easy to keep under control. Nature is a powerful enemy at times.'

She nodded and looked at Robinson.

'The house too needs much attention,' he said, reassured by her acceptance of Jacob's statement. 'But with few visitors now one has to question whether it is really of any importance.'

'Very tactfully put, both of you,' she said, 'if rather understated. The fact is that I have run out of money and cannot afford to run Warley Place. But I don't know what to do. I am tired and no longer feel able to carry on the fight.'

'We have been through difficult times before,' said Robinson, 'and we have always come through in the end.'

'Surviving, that is all,' she said wearily. 'But things will never be what they were, I have to accept that. It is simply not fair for you two to do almost on your own what a hundred people once did. Not just unfair, impossible.'

The two were silent for a minute. They had never heard her like this before, accepting defeat. She had always denied that there was a problem at all, let alone that it might be insurmountable.

'We could simply let the outer reaches go,' suggested Jacob. 'Just make sure that the parts near the house are kept as you wish them.'

'Would you let your alpine garden go, Jacob? Could you or I bear to see it revert to a weed infested wilderness?'

Jacob shook his head.

'And you, James, could you just let this house rot away? It's no use, I will have to sell.'

'No!' they both cried.

'Maybe at some stage someone will bring the garden back to its former glory,' she continued, 'but for now we will have to let go. The years of depression are over, the future looks promising. Perhaps someone will pay well for it. If they do I will instruct them to keep you, Jacob, to manage the gardens. You, James, will no doubt wish to retire but perhaps you could stay to manage the changeover for the new owner.'

'What about you, madam?' asked Jacob.

'I fear that I shall not survive the change for very long, but perhaps I shall end my days in one of the cottages doing my best not to interfere.'

'We have had some good times here,' said Robinson in an attempt to lighten the mood just a little. 'I have waited on the rich and famous, indeed on royalty. I have been left to run this house as I have wished, especially during your absences abroad. I would not have changed one single day of my life here.'

'And I have been able to oversee the development of the best alpine garden in Europe,' said Jacob. 'Nowhere else would I have had that opportunity. You have spared no expense in obtaining plants from all over the world. I too am glad to have had my time here, whatever may come.'

There was silence for a moment.

'Forgive me if I seem patronising,' continued Jacob. 'But perhaps best of all has been that I have worked alongside the great Miss Ellen Willmott.'

'Amen to that,' said Robinson.

'Your kind words are not deserved,' murmured their mistress, her eyes misting.

Jacob swallowed the last of his cheese and sipped his water.

'Would you do anything different?' asked Robinson.

'I have been too extravagant and would have been less so if it would have saved Warley Place,' she said, staring out through the conservatory window.

'I would like to thank you for all you have done,' she said, changing the subject abruptly as if annoyed at her uncharacteristic show of sentimentality. 'It has been a privilege to have you both working for me. Now I am a little tired and wish to retire early.'

The two men rose to their feet and Jacob walked to the door.

'Jacob,' said Ellen Willmott, following him.

He turned to her.

'Thank you,' she said.

He nodded, feeling his own eyes moistening and his throat tightening. She gave him a comforting smile and let him pick up his boots and continue on his way.

'Can I help, madam?' asked Robinson as Jacob trudged his way back to South Lodge.

'No, I will be fine. I have a little indigestion but nothing more. I would like to retire to my room now. But thank you for all you have done over these many years.'

She slowly made her way upstairs. Tired though she was, she slept badly that night and before dawn broke properly, she rose, restless and ill at ease. Going to the window she could see the trees emerging out of the early morning mist and the glow from the sun before it showed itself above the horizon. The beauty of the scene and the sound of the birds welcoming the dawn did nothing to lift her spirits.

She brought up a little wind. That was the trouble with eating cheese before going to bed. She even felt a little nauseous.

'I can never leave this place,' she said. 'Never.'

She started to sweat and clutched at the window sill to avoid falling.

She gasped as the indigestion tightened across her chest.

'Now I'll never have to,' she murmured to herself in sudden grateful realisation as the pain travelled down one arm. 'Perhaps there is a God.'

She crumpled to the floor.

The Mistress of Warley Place was dead.

Appendix 1
Bibliography

Books

Miss Willmott of Warley Place by Audrey le Lievre.
The original hardback version is no longer in print but is available from the public library. A softback version is available via the internet. It provided much of the background information for *The Wall*.

Warley Magna to Great Warley by George Harper.
This book is also an excellent reference source, both for Warley Place and for the wider history of the locality. It is also available in the public library.

Warley Place
This well illustrated Essex Wildlife Trust booklet is an excellent guide to the people, the fauna and the flora of Warley Place.

The Wall and *The Walnut Tree*
Ripples in a Pond is a sequel to these previous novels and although it can be read without reference to its predecessors, some references to previous events do occur.

La Mairie de Tresserve
An excellent book, in French but with English panels, about Ellen Willmott's home in France that is now the local Mairie.

Websites

www.essexwt.org.uk
This is the website of Essex Wildlife Trust. As well as providing information on all the EWT nature reserves and on wildlife in general it provides the information to enable you to become a member. Alternatively just ring 01621 862960 or call in at one of the visitor centres.

https://www.essexwt.org.uk/nature-reserves/warley-place
This is the section of the EWT website dealing with Warley Place.

http://www.spetchleygardens.co.uk/
Spetchley Park, near Worcester, is and was the home of the Berkeley family into which Rose Willmott, Ellen's sister, married. The gardens still exist and are well worth a visit.

Appendix 2
Tresserve

Tresserve is a delightful village near Aix-les-Bains, on the shores of Lac du Bourget, in South-East France. While visiting Aix-les-Bains for treatment for rheumatism at the local baths, Ellen Willmott and her sister Rose fell in love with the area, and with a chateau in Tresserve that was up for sale. In 1890 they bought it and they, together with relatives and friends, spent a lot of time there. Having visited it myself, I can understand why.

As is well known, Ellen Willmott's finances deteriorated rapidly as she spent all her money on plants, musical instruments, rare books and many other things, and as early as 1910 she seriously considered selling Warley Place and moving to her home at Tresserve. Fortunately for us she decided to stay, but eventually, in 1920, she was forced to sell her French home.

The house was originally bought by Lord Berkeley, then on his death and an uncertain few years, it ended up in public ownership and became the Mairie, or Town Hall, of Tresserve.

Ellen Willmott's name is far from forgotten there and a huge amount of work has been done by members of the *Association pour la Sauvegarde du Patrimoine de Tresserve* (an association safeguarding the heritage of Tresserve) in joining the Warley Place research group sorting and photographing Ellen Willmott's archived documents. A close and friendly relationship was very quickly established between us, and resulted in their visit to Warley Place and my own visit to Tresserve.

Appendix 3
Warley Place as it was

Although the map relates to 1904, it should be accurate enough to relate to the events in this book. A large scale version of this map is located in the Information Room at Warley Place.

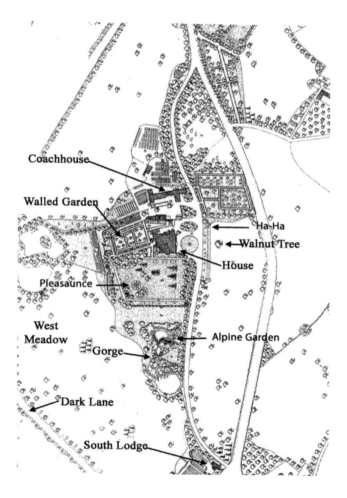